Doorways to the Unseen 7

6 Tales of Terror and Suspense

James Dermond

Ambages Books

This book is a work of fiction. The names, characters, organizations, places, events, and dialogue are either products of the author's imagination or are used in a fictitious manner.

ISBN: 978-1-946038-06-7

Cover art by Jeff Purnawan

"Deep into that darkness peering, long I stood there, wondering, fearing, doubting, dreaming dreams no mortal ever dared to dream before."

- 'The Raven' by Edgar Allan Poe

Contents

The Unearthly Gardens   1

The Plague   17

The Devil's Garden   33

Cast in Amber   49

A Hunger So...   69

Forged in Fire   83

About the Author   101

Postscript   103

The Unearthly Gardens

T homas let the chalky soil run out between his fingers and onto the barren ground at his sandaled feet. He looked out over the fields of pitted crops as they met the rolling hills outside his village and worried that this season's harvest might fail to feed his people.

The specter of famine loomed over Hometown for the first time in living memory. The previously rich soil of the farmlands surrounding the village elder's peaceful settlement was now dry and friable, unsuitable for planting and harvesting. With this harvest season at an end, the villagers came to fear starvation as their once-abundant crops were thin and mealy when finally collected and stored until the next harvest.

Thomas walked back from the fields to the meeting tent, its exterior modestly adorned, with an animal-hide flap hanging over the tent's entrance. He parted the leather curtain to step inside. The remaining village elders were assembled, seated on raised planks around the tent's stone-lined fire, the smoke drifting up through the structure's opening at its top into the early evening sky.

The chief elder had called a council and invited the village shaman as well, lest the harvest gods be insulted. The holy man also claimed that he possessed some insight into why the crops had failed when they had so recently seemed ripe for a successful harvest.

"The land itself has been cursed. Our soil has been poisoned by an outsider." Elijah, the village shaman, gestured over the tent's open fire with both hands, his weathered face lit from beneath by the light of the burning branches. "We

1

have brought this tragedy upon ourselves. Impiety among the youth, lack of observance, there are so many ways to attract the wrath of the gods."

The elders observed his mildly theatrical performance and then Thomas spoke to the shaman, as if interrogating him, "If you believe that someone caused the soil to go sour, how can we find him? Where is this magician that can taint our land so quickly and without warning?"

Elijah became still, leaning on his ornate wooden staff, his voice low as he answered Thomas, "I saw him— or perhaps it—at the edge of the forest past the farmers' plots more than two moons ago. Before our crops began to wither.

"I wasn't sure if it was a man or a spirit, but it was a dark shadow against the full moon, covered from head to foot. The cloaked one stood on the hill and looked over the crops, not moving save for the nighttime winds rustling its long garment. I watched from a distance before he vanished in the blink of an eye; only a spirit of the forest could do something like that. Sinister magic is working against our people."

A village elder seated next to Elijah stood and looked over the men present, "My son, Lucas, saw the same spirit, not long after Elijah. As Elijah said, the shrouded spirit-man perched on the closest hill near the crops and watched in darkness, only to suddenly disappear after a short while. That the crops began to die not long after the spirit's visits can't be just ill fortune."

Elijah prodded the fire with his staff, his bare arms wizened and desiccated. "Some searchers could go into the forest, find the spirit and dispel it, removing the curse on the soil. Hometown may not survive past the next harvest season if we don't act boldly and soon." Elijah seemed very withdrawn as he spoke, as if he could sense the foreboding descending over the council of elders and what might become of him if his plea was rejected.

Thomas gazed over the crackling fire at Elijah and replied, "The Old Ways forbid us from journeying more than three leagues into the depths of the forest. Even a shaman can't change the laws passed down to us by the Ancestors. We might just have to make a sacrifice of forest beasts to the harvest gods instead, profane youth notwithstanding."

Thomas wasn't sure if Elijah had picked up on his veiled jibe or not. Elijah returned Thomas's gaze coolly. "The Ancestors also passed down obligations to thrive and to grow Hometown, to keep this place a haven for our people. If the source of the corruption dwells in the forest, then searchers must go into the forest to find it. Preserving the Old Ways mean nothing if we are all dead."

The elders murmured among themselves, and then the chief elder, Jacob, stood and spoke, "It is settled. Thomas, choose four searchers from among our best men. The searchers must travel past the three leagues threshold and explore the forest beyond the boundary set by the Ancestors. This spiteful spirit may be there and can be thwarted if found. We may starve after the next harvest if the searchers fail to find what is causing the land to die beneath our very feet."

Jacob was said to be a direct descendent of the Ancestors, a man of considerable height and prodigious strength despite his advanced age. His father and his father before him had led Hometown and its inhabitants through many trials, but nothing as dire as what had come upon them with the failure of this harvest. Jacob now began to feel a gnawing dread that he would be the last of his line if the searchers were not successful in their quest.

Jerod entered his family's tent, placing a clutch of game birds strung together by their feet onto its earthen floor. Jerod's wife, Sara, was swaddling their infant son, setting him down for the night in his crib as Jerod greeted her with the eventide greeting.

"Not as many as I had hoped." Jerod hung his bow and quiver near the tent's entrance. "Gage only fell two this hunt. Lara may not even let him back inside their tent tonight." Jerod attempted to make light of their situation, but even he was beginning to worry about the dearth of animal life in the woods near the village. Birds and other small game had started to grow scarce not long after the farmers noticed the failure of this season's crops.

"Samuel's asleep now. Come lie with me." Sara lay on her side across their bed of animal skins, inviting Jerod to join her by running a hand over the soft covers nearest to her. Jerod removed his hunter's jerkin and lay facing his wife, caressing her hair as she continued speaking.

Sara put on a wry expression, the corners of her eyes crinkling slightly. "Do they know why the hunts are failing? What have the elders said? Elijah may have to make an offering to the gods or there will soon be no game left." The women of Hometown had gathered earlier that day outside the fields as they worked, discussing the lack of recent success in the hunts.

Jerod turned onto his back and looked up into the opening in the tent's ceiling, the stars overhead drifting through the evening sky. "No, none of the elders seem to know, or at least they haven't told any searchers or hunters. The village council had a meeting today while we were returning from the forest, so they might tell us something tomorrow. I can never tell with them."

There was the sound of someone moving outside the tent. Jerod sat up, reaching for his jerkin and boots. He dressed quickly, then crept toward the veil of skins sheltering the tent's interior. "Jerod, I need to speak with you. Step outside." Thomas spoke quietly, but the urgency in his voice was unmistakable.

Jerod turned to look at his wife, who was now standing on their bed, then parted the skin flaps to venture into the cool air of the village evening from the warmth of his tent. Thomas stood close to the tent, watching Jerod as he turned to face him. "Walk with me. The council of elders has made a decision."

Jerod briefly glanced at the tent's entrance, then followed Thomas away from his dwelling, down the path between the tents of the people to the now-deserted meeting place of the elders. The two men stood alone, and Thomas reached out to touch Jerod's shoulder in confidence.

"Jacob has tasked me with choosing four men from among the people to go past the lands set by the Ancestors. Elijah and the elders believe that we are being cursed by a malevolent spirit, and this is why the crops fail. The spirit must make its home in the far forest and can be banished there."

Jerod searched Thomas's weary eyes, unsure of how to answer him. "How can anyone change what was given to us with the Old Ways? There could be nothing but death waiting for us in the forest. The Ancestors laid down those laws to keep the people from unnecessary harm."

Thomas replied matter-of-factly, "The council has decided. The Ancestors are not here to complain. I will tell Gage that he will accompany you as well, along with two others." Jerod felt a shiver pass over him as the traditions he was raised with from birth were being toppled around him. To hear one of the elders dismiss generations of his people's customs with a wave of his hand sorely troubled the typically stoic Jerod.

"How will we fight the forest spirit if we are able to find it? Gage and I are hunters, not shamans. We have no magic."

Thomas again seemed unconcerned as he answered Jerod. "Elijah will ward all of you against evil spirits. The spirit of the forest takes the shape of a man, so he can be harmed by those with the ward. So says Elijah."

Thomas walked back to his family tent after reassuring Jerod, asking him to sleep well before leaving in the morning. However, Thomas's outer indifference masked his own trepidation. He thought back to his father and the stories he'd told Thomas.

The people had lived their entire lives within the valley, as did everyone before them. The sun, the moon, the sky, the valley, and the forest behind the valley were the entire world. The gods lived in the sky, and in the sun and the moon. The edge of the forest was where the world ended for the people, and what lay beyond was the rest of the world.

In the time of the Ancestors, there was terrible pain and hardship, but the Ancestors created Hometown for the people to keep them safe. The people would never have to suffer if Hometown remained their refuge, with the Old Ways directing how the people should live. The Ancestors gave stern warning about the deep forest past Hometown and made this as their First Law. Thomas had never doubted the First Law before, but now wondered from what the Ancestors were trying to protect the people.

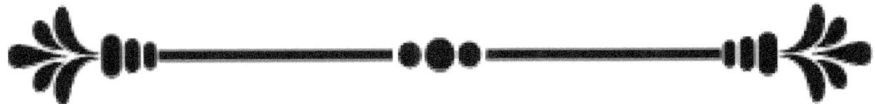

Elijah dabbed the ochre paint in several stripes over Jerod's chiseled face, the mixture rapidly drying in the smoky, heated air of the meeting tent. The village elders and the shaman had assembled again, but this time with the family members of the four searchers chosen to venture into the deep forest. Jerod's father and mother stood solemnly as Elijah finished applying the spirit wards from a ceremonial bowl to the other three searchers' faces, hopeful that their only son's sacred quest would save Hometown but also fearful they may never see him again.

The men armed themselves with fire-hardened wooden spears, sinew-strung bows, and flint-tipped arrows, clad only in the roughest of leathers. The band of searchers planned to set out on foot to explore the uncharted wilderness in the hopes of identifying the evil, or at least finding a new source of food for the village if all else failed. Jerod was chosen to lead the other young men, having honed his tracking skills over several summers of hunts in the sparser forestlands on the outskirts of Hometown.

The shaman chanted over the band as they stood before him. "The gods' blessings be upon you. Go forth and find that which threatens our people. Go forth and find that which will heal our soil and return us to abundance. Let it be so." Elijah waved a smoldering clay censer before the searchers, stuffed with flowering plants that had been grown in his own tent, the plants' aroma wrapping the men in a mist as a shield of protection.

Jerod thought that he had never placed much credence in the gods before today, but now was not a time to doubt their divinity. If Jerod returned alive from this anointed quest, that would be enough proof of their existence to him.

The searchers left Hometown under the bright morning sun, following the single path that wound through the villagers' dwellings, the grain storehouse built from wooden poles and clay, and the meeting place of the elders, then past the fields to the mostly unknown forest.

The dense forest with its towering trees and thick overgrowth in the distance had never held much mystery for the people of Hometown as none had ever thought of traversing the compact parameter set for hunting and for the gathering of wild plants. The Old Ways and its strictures had forbidden anyone from the journey now being undertaken, and no one had ever dared to do otherwise.

Several hours of vigorous walking were enough to leave behind the familiar woods and breach the limits imposed by the Ancestors. The trees here in the deep forest were taller and more knotted than those within the reaches of Hometown, revealing a storied natural history in lands where no one had set foot before. The band of men were soon immersed in the primeval forest, awed by its savage beauty and inscrutable nature.

The searchers took a short rest by a running stream, Jerod drinking carefully from its waters. Jerod studied his men as they reclined by the riparian banks, taking a meal of barley bread.

His mind wandered to his wife and infant son, recalling Samuel's birth just six moons ago. The midwife had delivered the baby, judging him to be sound and healthy. Thomas had once remarked that in the time of the Ancestors, newborn babies were judged as many were found sick and the shamans then had to "return them to the gods."

The band resumed its march up a sharp incline, finally reaching a vista in the forest's plateau. Arthur stopped behind Jerod and gestured to him, with Gage and Sean pausing to see what Arthur wanted. Arthur had a curious character and seemed too glib for a searcher, at least in Jerod's mind. Arthur might have been better suited as a shaman.

Arthur said, "Jerod, that colorful bird sitting on the branch ahead of us, do you see it?"

Jerod removed his leather pack and placed it on the forest floor. "Where? I don't see anything."

Arthur replied, "Look directly ahead and then up, you'll see it."

Jerod rubbed the back of his neck and peered ahead into the quiet mass of trees surrounding them. There, on a high branch, was a kind of bird he had never encountered before. Unlike the drab feathers worn by the fowl hunted for the village roasts, this bird sported bright red-and-yellow plumage, its wings spreading generously as it lifted itself from its perch and glided deeper into the leafy foliage of the forest.

Jerod was surprised, but not overly concerned. "I'm sure we'll run into some odd things as we make progress. No one's ever been here; it's untouched by the people. A bird is probably the least we have to worry ourselves about."

Jerod put his arms through his pack's straps after lifting it from the ground and continued walking ahead of the others. Arthur shrugged, resuming his pace behind Jerod, but turning around to possibly spy the strange bird that seemed so out-of- place in the green-and-brown hues of the forest's landscape.

The unwearied searchers reached what Jerod believed to be the heart of the forest as the sun began to wane, its slow voyage across the horizon spilling light over the tops of the trees and onto the forest floor. Still, however, the ground beneath this part of the forest was almost entirely obscured by the colossal trees' thick canopy, shafts of sunlight only piercing through sporadically.

Jerod and his band came for a short rest in a clearing amidst the ancient trees. Here in the woodland twilight, an astonishing flower bloomed, blood-red in color and sickeningly sweet in scent.

Jerod stood over the band's disturbing discovery, noting that this bizarre flower might have been cultivated by hand as no other plants grew near it on the forest floor. The soil around the peculiar flower also appeared to be withered, as if the flower was somehow leeching more than just its natural sustenance.

"Now this is something we should worry about," Arthur noted as he turned to look at Jerod. "This flower looks dangerous, possibly deadly. Do you think it was planted here by the spirit of the forest?"

Jerod looked back at Gage and Sean, who were keeping their distance as they sat on a patch of grass near the trees lining the clearing. "I can't say," Jerod replied. "We shouldn't try to pick it, even though Elijah would probably treasure it. Just leave the flower alone and we will keep moving until sundown. This isn't a good place to make camp, not even considering that flower."

The band continued its trek through the tangled forest until the dimming sun made it impossible to go further. Jerod decided to make camp against what appeared to be the sheer side of a cliff, the view of the rocks above concealed by the trees.

Sturdy ivy vines grew everywhere on the stone wall, hanging down around the band as they built a fire from broken tree branches and settled in for the night. Jerod placed Gage on nighttime watch, the other searchers falling asleep in the soft glow of the campfire.

Gage grumbled as he felt the need for sleep, resenting that Sean was able to rest first before taking the second guard shift. The band had seen no large animals in the forest, and predators bigger than a feral pig did not exist in their experience, but Jerod wished to take no risks. What might be found in the untamed forest at night could surprise them in unpleasant ways.

Some time in silence passed, and then Gage heard a humming sound in the distance, steadily growing louder. Could it be that funny bird the band saw before? No, this sounded like something much larger than a bird, and it was getting closer. Gage squatted next to Jerod's slumbering form and prodded him awake.

"Jerod, wake up, quick. Something is coming." Jerod rolled over on his woven fiber mat and squinted at Gage. "This had better be serious," Jerod muttered sleepily.

Arthur and Sean hid in the high bushes with Jerod and Gage, not far from the campsite, its small fire now buried under a mound of dirt. The moonlight provided some visibility, but only a faint outline of the forest flora in front of the band could be perceived without the light of the campfire.

As the men stared out into the dark forest, a silvery sphere the size of a harvest cart floated downward, facing the side of the cliff where they'd made camp as the sphere made its descent from above the trees.

The sphere hovered in place before the ivy-covered surface. A clicking noise was heard, and the stone wall parted into two sections with a nearly silent hiss, revealing the alcove situated behind it.

Brilliant, intense light flooded out from the newly exposed enclosure, illuminating the nighttime forest, and casting the sphere's shadow over the hiding place of the searchers. The silvery object then flew up into an open shaft in the ceiling of a room that was now visible, the uncovered doorway within the cliff beginning to slide shut again.

"That could be the resting place of the spirit of the forest. We have to chase that cart, or whatever it is, inside the cliff." Jerod immediately stood and ran toward the two pieces of the wall as they continued to close.

The others hesitated, but then Arthur rose from behind the bushes and ran after Jerod, so Gage and Sean followed. The men gathered in a featureless white room the length and breadth of a half-score of tents, cool air drifting out of the open shaft in the room's ceiling where the flying cart had disappeared. The wall of the cliff closed behind them, blocking egress to the forest.

Jerod examined the shaft and then reached into his pack once he had set it down on the cold floor. Jerod removed a fiber rope and slung it over the length of his arms.

"The only way is up through that opening," Jerod observed. "This should be something like scaling the rocky hillsides near Hometown. I didn't think the forest spirit would find rest in the heavens. I thought that underground was more likely."

Jerod swung the rope and caught a strut protruding from the shiny tube at the mouth of the shaft, its hard bone hook attached to the end of the rope. The tube was made of a material the searchers had never seen before but appeared to be something like that of the flying cart.

Jerod tugged at the rope to make sure it was secure. "I'll go first. If I make it to the opening, climb up behind me." Jerod easily scaled the rope, reaching the first strut of the tube that lined the shaft walls, his flowing hair stirred by the circulating air swirling around him.

There were more struts evenly spaced along the side of the tube facing him, and Jerod began to make his way up the shaft to what he hoped would be the top. Gage observed Jerod from the floor and then grasped the dangling rope with his rugged hands, pulling himself to the first strut.

Jerod glanced down and saw that he had made good progress up the tube's shaft. Gage, Arthur, and Sean were gaining on him but appeared small in the distance. Jerod steadied himself, as the scope of the ascent was much greater than he had anticipated. The height he had reached was daunting and could easily cause vertigo in someone less resolute.

The shaft enveloping the tube was as brightly lit as the noonday sun, but Jerod could see no torch or lantern of any kind as he clambered his way up the struts.

Jerod grabbed the last strut before the top of the metallic tube and then hauled himself through its circular opening. He rested for a moment on another cold, smooth floor like the one at the bottom of the shaft, the room as white and featureless as before.

Looking around, Jerod noted that this room was more spacious than the first, with the addition of a single closed door at its far end. In the ceiling of the room, suspended above the metal tube in its own shimmering shaft, was a gray cylinder with many blinking-colored lights, large enough to accommodate several people.

Jerod brought himself to his feet and walked cautiously toward the closed door. The door opened with a whooshing sound as Jerod grew close, disappearing into the wall supporting it.

Jumping back, the unexpected movement startled Jerod. He could see no one on the other side to open the door so suddenly. Jerod breathed deeply of the lush fragrance now washing over him as he took a step forward. What he saw through the open door was an entirely new world, completely outside of his unrefined imagination.

The clatter of Gage reaching the top of the shaft broke Jerod out of his near trance-like state upon seeing the unearthly garden laid out before him. The botanical garden was vast and expansive, marble statuary adorning its avenues and pathways. A cobbled stone path led from the white room's door to a far-off circle at the garden's center.

"Jerod, what do you see?" Gage stood next to Jerod and placed a hand over his brow, the hazy sun from the orange-lit horizon momentarily blinding him. Arthur and Sean joined their fellows at the door, the men deciding to explore the alien setting despite its inherent uncertainty.

The flora and fauna of the garden was unlike any they'd ever seen. Vividly colored insect life fluttered about while enormous, polychromatic birds glided languidly overhead as the searchers strode down the stone path. Everywhere they turned was a new sight, an unfamiliar shade, or an unimagined creature.

"There's the red-and-yellow bird we saw in the forest. Wait. There's three of them by that stone figure." Arthur pointed along the path to a statute of a bare-chested man posing with a shield and spear. The birds rested on the branch of a fruit-bearing tree in full bloom, one bordering the pathway leading toward the center.

Jerod posited, "That bird must've escaped down the tunnel we climbed up. Or maybe the spirit of the forest left it there. This has to be where he makes his home, or else we are in Heaven." Jerod turned to look at his men, but they did not answer him, their eyes wide, attempting to absorb the sensory excess around them.

The searchers came to the central circle, where a synthetic white marble kiosk stood alone, somewhat obscured by light overgrowth from the garden's intrusions over time. Within the empty space of the kiosk's interior was the indentation of a human hand, the impressions of its five fingers splayed evenly around the palm.

"This looks like something the gods would leave for their devoted." Jerod reached out to touch the handprint, but then hesitated, pulling back.

Arthur said, "I'll touch it for you. We might even summon the gods. Wish me luck."

Jerod moved aside, and Arthur reached down to the surface of the kiosk's interior, pressing his own hand firmly into the molding. Flickering blue light filled the vacant space within, and a startled Arthur took a few steps back, bumping into his comrades.

The transparent image of a man dressed in elaborate, tailored clothes took shape over the handprint and began to speak to the searchers, his voice distant and hollow:

"Welcome to the Unearthly Gardens, Deck Eight of the Starship Daedalus. I am the Curator of the botanical gardens, which are modeled after the famed Orto Botanico di Padova. Here, however, we are dedicated to presenting new forms of life which are not indigenous to Old Terra but have been developed exclusively by Strasburger-Ming Industrial Genetics for transport to our eventual destination in the Delta Orionis star system. Please enjoy your visit to these gardens and find peace at this lush oasis in space."

The image of the Curator flickered off and the garden became eerily silent once more, without so much as the sound of a chirping bird. Jerod took on a worried expression and said, "Was that a spirit, or maybe a god? It could have been a vision made from this weird rock. Or maybe it's just magic."

Arthur reassured him, "It's gone now. Some of what the little man said sounded like the words we use, but most of it was only noise. The man did say 'peace,' so this could be a holy place to the gods."

The band wandered among the stagnant fountains and ill-maintained, columnated buildings of the garden, following the stone path to the circular garden's far end. Resting at the path's destination was a glass-paneled building, its exterior frosted from disuse.

"There is a door, but why can we see into the house? Is this magic stone too?" Arthur stepped forward and touched the doorknob of the solitary door leading inside the orchid greenhouse.

The knob was coated with a wet film of some sort that was sticky to his skin and burned slightly. The band entered and was briefly overwhelmed by the thick, humid atmosphere. Orange sunlight filtered weakly through the opaque glass rooftop, dimly lighting the rows of plants spilling out over the walkways.

"This is the farmlands of the gods," Sean said once he had surveyed the open room with its many flowering orchids.

"The gods eat flowers, Sean?" Arthur smirked.

Gage looked down over a row of orchids not far from the doorway after he had walked away from the group.

"That blood flower from the forest is here, too. There is a whole plot of them here."

Jerod stood next to Gage and examined the flower that he had feared touching before. "This is it. The sickly smelling flower that saps the woodlands with its roots. The forest spirit can't be far, my friends."

Arthur called to his fellows from another area of the greenhouse, "I found something too. There is a workplace back here. There are some tools I recognize, but they aren't made of wood or stone. Come and see for yourselves."

At the back of the greenhouse, away from most of the plant life, was a workshop with several synthetic wood tables. The tables, as with the rest of the gardens, were long-neglected and strewn with tools and instruments such as those used in scientific research.

On one of the tables was a plastic tablet with a lid that opened when unlatched. Arthur picked up the tablet and unfastened its lid, placing the lid in the upright position.

As before in the garden, a muted blue light flickered and the holographic image of a man who resembled the Curator appeared on the inner surface as Arthur held it in front of him. The man began to speak, his voice hollow as it had been at the marble kiosk:

"Holo-journal log number 2290-AUG08. I am incrementally adjusting to this new body that was provided by my employers. I agreed to undergo this procedure to have my conscious mind and my memories imprinted into this artificial facsimile of my youthful self. This construct will allow me to make the lengthy trip to the colonization planet without the need to enter a suspension capsule.

"Most of the crew members and civilian colonists are held in these cryo-capsules, frozen in a state of suspended animation for the duration of the decades-long journey. While the others sleep, I will manage the Unearthly Gardens and continue with my botany studies undisturbed."

The image of the man flickered for a moment, and he then began speaking again, this time dressed in a white lab coat:

"Holo-journal log number 2290-AUG27. Attempted cross-pollination between the two orchid species detailed in holo-journal entry 2289-SEP13. Crosspollination failed to result in a new hybrid species as intended. I will select two new orchid species and reattempt the cross-pollination process, this time isolating for genetic robustness. With more than thirty thousand species and over seventy thousand cultivars, identifying new candidates for cross-pollination should not be an issue."

The image of the man flickered again, but for a few minutes instead of several seconds, as if the tablet was struggling to function correctly. Once the man reappeared and began speaking, his voice sounded panicked, afraid:

"Holo-journal log number 2290-DEC08. There has been a disaster onboard the Daedalus. I have lost contact with the upper decks, and no visitors or human grounds crew have returned since the sudden shock to the vessel.

"The floor of the lab shook violently, with some of my fragile plants being crushed by the falling debris from the greenhouse roof. The grounds of the gardens and my workspace were then bathed in an unnatural light, emitting a dreadful yellow glow for some time after this unexpected catastrophe. I am not sure of the nature of the disaster, but I fear the worst."

The image of the man vanished briefly and then returned, his voice stuttering slightly as the avatar flickered in and out:

"Holo-journal log number 2291-MAR11. The long-term health of the garden's flora and fauna is in question after the event. Cellular testing has confirmed that most, if not all, of the lifeforms in the gardens have been altered in some manner after last year's cataclysm. Certain flowering plants have become very aggressive; I have placed these plants on an observation list that is being updated continually.

"I am not sure what the cosmic rays may have done to me as well. My artificial body should be most durable, but that does not seem to be the case. I grow more fatigued with each passing week, more sensitive to sounds and motion outside of my greenhouse. There are plants— carnivorous plants—that I would swear are whispering to me while I tend the gardens. These plants are demanding more food than what I already give them...new kinds of food."

The image of the man flickered and then skipped around, with no intelligible words as he spoke. The tablet stabilized and the man spoke once again, but his appearance was altered from the previous entries. Now, he wore a long cloak, and his hands were not visible:

"Holo-journal log number 2292-OCT21. I have found a solution to the food problem, but it will require the use of the ecology drones stored on Decks Six and Seven. Garden drones presently maintain the Unearthly Gardens and other areas of the ship, but exposure to radiation from the disaster has made their operation unstable. Further cultivation of the Nepenthes rajah hybrid will require securing more drones and more growing space on other decks, some of which seem to be inhabited by survivors."

The holo-journal's final entry recorded no date, and the Curator's face was hidden from view as he spoke, his body covered entirely by the long cloak. His voice had also changed, becoming very thin, even inhuman:

"The drones from the upper decks have been successfully reprogrammed and can now extract mineral wealth from soil in addition to replenishing nutrient depleted soil as was intended with the drones' original programming. The additional nutrients and the other newly acquired food sources will feed it and allow me to join with it to survive on this ship. The only obstacle now is determining a method of shutting down the day and night cycle on the inhabited decks so that it won't be harmed due to the organism's susceptibility to sunlight, even the ship's artificial sunlight."

After the last entry finished, the tablet powered down, its power cell spent. Arthur placed the tablet on the worktable in front of him and saw that his fellows were as badly shaken as he was by the Curator's tale, those parts that could be understood by the searchers.

"Do you smell that?" Arthur then noted the sickeningly sweet odor that they had first inhaled in the forest, which was faintly noticeable in the greenhouse before but was now much stronger. In the gloomy light of the decaying greenhouse, Jerod and his fellows saw a cloaked figure standing silently in the aisle facing them, between the rows of flowering plants.

The figure glided effortlessly towards the band, a rustling sound perceptible along with the overpowering scent of orchids. The figure's cloak opened wide as it approached, and fibrous, tentacled appendages ending in open mouths full of serrated teeth writhed toward the searchers. The last sound Jerod heard was Arthur screaming in terror...

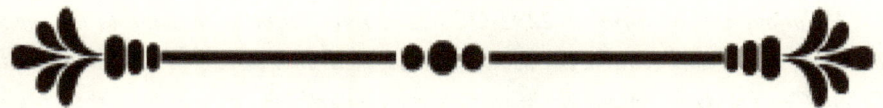

Thomas had returned to where the fields met the gentle hills outside of Hometown, the diffuse rays of the late afternoon sun basking over the village. The elders believed that Jerod's band of searchers was lost for good.

Weeks had passed, and they had failed to return from the quest. Elijah attempted to divine their whereabouts, and then suggested sending another expedition, but the council of elders voted it down.

The village's foodstuffs were dwindling faster than anticipated and would not last until the next harvest. Thomas looked up into the mild, sunny sky and noticed something odd. The sun above the village settlement and farmlands seemed to fade very briefly and then refocus, shining once again. Thomas squinted, careful not to look directly into the sun's orb. It happened yet again.

Then, an abrupt darkness. Thomas stumbled about in a panic, the distant cries of the villagers echoing into the void. Thomas inhaled. The sickeningly sweet smell of orchids seeped into the village like a miasma, the only thing discernable in the eternal night of Hometown.

The Plague

"Rise and shine, Bartholomew."

Bart awoke while lying on his side. His freshly exfoliated face pointed at the wall paneling along the side of his bed as he felt the sting of adjusting his eyesight to a new morning after a night of sleep. Bart remained curled up under the cotton sheets, listening to his grandmother make her way around the room behind him. His nose wrinkled at a scent that he recognized but that was out of place indoors.

Bart felt some fingers touch his back. "Bartholomew, it is time to get up and do your chores. Don't be a lazybones. Your mother and sister need those bales brought down for the livestock." Granny's voice was unusually hoarse, almost as if she had been through a harsh bout of coughing.

Bart rolled over and gazed into his grandmother's face, which was now hovering close to his. Her features appeared blurry, and Bart squinted to focus on what was in front of him. He saw two gaping wounds where Granny's eyes should have been instead, set in her otherwise unmarred countenance.

Granny rasped, "Bartholomew, it's past daybreak, and your help is needed. I'll fix you some breakfast, and then it's off with you to your chores. Don't keep them waiting any longer."

Bart rolled over and bolted up, pushing himself against the wall behind his bed, the palms of his hands flat against its surface. He watched his grandmother motion her head back and forth as if searching for him; Granny seemed oblivious to her injury and just kept talking. "Bartholomew, where did you go? Are you getting yourself ready? I'll be downstairs in the kitchen making some eggs."

Granny stood from where she had knelt at the side of Bart's bedframe and began shuffling past the oaken study desk and stainless-steel coat rack, which were situated by the bedroom window. She was headed toward the bedroom door, her somewhat stooped form keeping its slow pace forward.

When Granny reached the threshold of the open doorway, she paused and looked to her side to speak, "Bartholomew, are you coming or not?" Granny remained motionless, with the profile of her head turned toward him as if waiting for Bart's response.

Bart was able to inspect Granny more closely as she stood in the doorway and saw that her floral apron was covered in bloody stains. Bart had noticed a pungent odor when he first became conscious, but now everything was fully registering following his sudden shock into wakefulness. He could also discern the handle of a butcher knife sticking out of Granny's left apron pocket with a deep red blot formed over the pocket's cloth.

Bart reflexively placed a hand over his mouth to muffle the involuntary scream he almost produced. His mind was racing, and he had trouble forming coherent thoughts. "Has Granny gone crazy? Where are Mom and Sis?" Bart lowered his hand and decided silently, "I have to make it outside. They can't be in the house unless Granny has already gotten to them."

His sneakers were under the base of the bed's headboard. Bart crept around the edge of the bedframe, reached down, and then put them on without tying the laces. He quietly stepped toward Granny and then inched his way to the narrow space between her and the outside hallway of the family home's upstairs floor. Bart could now see from his room that the cream-painted wooden rails leading up the stairs were smeared everywhere with blood.

"Bartholomew?" Granny stepped into the hallway past the bedroom's interior. Her back was now facing the room, and Bart slid past her and the bedroom door. He stopped his progress when he saw that Granny was reaching for the butcher knife in her apron pocket. Granny turned around so that she was facing the bedroom door with the knife drawn and said again, "Bartholomew?"

Bart leapt for the bathroom at the end of the hall, not risking the stairs. The bathroom door was slightly ajar, and Bart threw himself into the small space, surreptitiously locking the door behind him. He pressed himself against the door's white-coated paint, shut his eyes, and took long, deep breaths, before backing away to stand in the bathroom's center next to the sink.

Granny was walking around in the hall at what sounded like the top of the stairway; she didn't seem to be coming toward him. She called out to Bart, "I can't find my glasses, Bartholomew. Help me find my glasses."

Bart glanced down and saw two gouged eyeballs in the bathroom sink and a pair of bloody medical scissors on the counter. The shower curtain was in tatters and had been slashed in several places, while the bathroom floor was littered with tissue paper and other toiletries. Someone had been seized by an apoplectic fit in here and then torn into everything around them. Bart tied his sneaker's checkerboard laces and prepared himself for the climb down from the bathroom window.

He pushed up the lower half of the double hung window frame after undoing the latch at its middle. Bart stuck his head out the window and did a cursory survey of the grounds around his family's farmhouse.

He could see a thick pillar of pitch smoke reaching up into the otherwise clear summer sky from over the hills at Cassville, which was miles away from the family home. As the farmhouse had no immediate neighbors, Bart could observe nothing else and acted to fall from the second-story window.

He lowered himself by his hands from the window's opening until he was flush against the farmhouse's gray siding. Bart dangled briefly from the windowsill and then let go. He fell the short length to the ground and landed in the grass, making a quick recovery to stand on his feet. The smoke over the horizon had now become more prominent with multiple spires twisting in the wind, forming a tenebrous umbrella over the town.

Bart turned the old farmhouse's side corner from his bedroom window to its front and could then view the occupant of the broad porch that buffered the farmhouse's weathered doorway.

There was a figure seated in a rocking chair, rhythmically swaying with the balmy halcyon breeze. Bart's father sat in the chair with his head on his lap. The man's overalls were drenched in blood, and the head lay on its side with its eyes open, staring in Bart's direction but comprehending nothing. Bart summoned the strength to move forward and then kept walking, past the opposite front corner of the farmhouse to the barn, which was out in back.

Bart could hear the familiar sound of an axe hitting a log as his mother and sister entered his field of vision. Piles of timber were near the open double doors of the blue barn, but none of them was being struck. Bart's mother was, instead, removing his sister's left arm below the elbow with a chopping axe; the arm was partially cleaved but remained attached despite Mom's efforts. His teenage sister was standing over a tree stump bent at the waist, holding her arm out, while Mom laid another blow, this time severing the arm completely.

The mangled arm fell off the stump into the gore-splattered dirt surrounding it. Bart's sister staggered a bit, corrected herself to stand upright, and then beamed from ear to ear. Both women giggled obscenely, while Mom handed Sis the axe, before kneeling down at the stump and extending her own left arm over its surface. Their faces were markedly streaked with cruor, in the pattern of dried tears.

Mom glimpsed Bart when she turned her head and abruptly snapped up from her spot at the stump. Both women let out a bizarre keening in unison, their expressions glazed with madness, red-rimmed eyes blazing with an almost religious fanaticism.

Mom grabbed the axe from Sis and dashed at Bart with the weapon raised over her head. Sis followed, waving her amputated limb before her, a thin stream of blood blotting the mowed grass beneath her feet as she ran.

Bart lurched and sprinted in the direction of the highway, which passed the boundary of the farm's crop fields. He didn't dare look behind as he ran—his family members seemed to possess almost preternatural speed. Bart ran faster than he had ever run in his life, even as the thumping tracks behind him faded into the distance.

The highway was empty once Bart reached its paved lanes, and he continued to run. He passed a car that had been abandoned in a ditch, its emergency lights blinking from the tail end that faced the highway from its resting place. Boxes were tied to a rack on the car roof, the supplies of whoever had tried to leave Cassville but had failed.

Bart started to come to a halt only after his lungs began to burn from their exertion. He stumbled and sat himself in the gravel on the side of the highway, regaining his breath after a while, and then sobbing at his loss. Mom and Sis were long gone behind him.

Bart continued to sit at the periphery of the highway, his arms resting over his crossed knees, his brain reeling from all that had transpired. "My God, what is going on? They were mutilating themselves. The same thing must be happening in Cassville." He looked over the pastureland from his vantage point on the road and could see no one else.

As Bart dusted himself off to continue, pressure began building in his right ear, causing him to rub it in hopes of clearing the sensation. The pressure spread to his left ear, and a subdued, sinusoidal humming then became noticeable. The pulsating hum started to overwhelm the ambient noise of the outside and fill Bart's skull with a mounting, nearly unbearable tension.

"Ahhhh…" Bart tried to speak, but no words came forth. The pulsating hum clouded his sight, with the hills, the fields, and the highway being replaced by a brilliant white light.

Bart fell over, hitting the tarred curb, clasping both his ears with his hands. The humming became a dull but all-consuming buzz, so loud as to preclude cerebration. Bart clenched his teeth in agony and continued to shield his ears, in a vain effort to block out the roaring ocean of sound.

Then it stopped. His back was bruised from where he had fallen on the curb, but he was able to sit up in a daze. Bart could feel something moist on his skin, so he touched his cheek. A small amount of blood had flowed from his right eye socket and formed a rivulet across his face, which was now dripping onto his T-shirt.

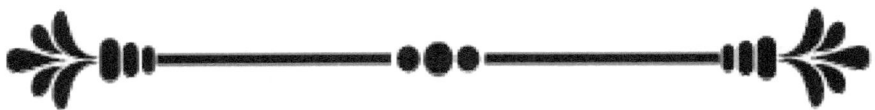

The sun was at its golden hour when Bart passed the "Welcome to Cassville—One Great City" sign after the highway exit. The dimming sun's radiance from behind the stylized, antiquated sign was adequate enough to view the buildings below the off ramp from the highway, which showed evidence of extensive looting and vandalism. Bart could see no movement from either cars or townspeople as he descended the highway's off ramp to the town's main street.

The exit to town was blocked by a pile up of burned-out cars that were smoldering and exuded a gasoline smell, around which were strewn glass shards and the contents of luggage from fleeing passengers. Bart did not want to peer into the car seats as he walked by, for fear of what he might witness.

"Everyone is gone. Not a soul alive in Cassville," Bart whispered to himself. The bright pink exterior walls of the Hen's Roost Diner were blacked by fire, with every one of its windows broken in. As with the highway scene, the cars in the parking lot had been torched, doors welded together by the intensity of the heat.

Bart stood on the steps of the Hen's Roost, which were strewn with debris from whatever carnage had taken place there. The patron booths and the countertop were no longer fully visible, as they had been partially buried in emptied boxes and broken items from the kitchen. Bart stepped inside through the open door and could smell that the diner's grill had recently been used to cook some kind of meat in apparently large quantities.

The double doors to the back kitchen area were open and had been splattered with gore that was now drying but still gave off a strong odor mixed in with the cooked meat and burning diesel smell. Bart pushed his way into the back kitchen and then saw all of them.

Bodies were stacked up in several piles, reaching to the kitchen ceiling. There must have been fifty people in those piles. Limbs had been hacked off, and many of the bodies had been eviscerated. Those corpses that were still whole had been contorted into abnormal, almost impossible shapes, feeding the grotesque nature of the scene.

Bart felt a strong sense of fear upon seeing what had happened and could now guess where the grilled flesh from the diner had been obtained. The floor was sticky and wet with blood draining into the grates between the commercial sinks that had been used as an abattoir. Bart opened the door of the walk-in freezer connected to the kitchen and saw that several more bodies had been hung on hooks, with plastic bags of body parts and internal organs stacked on metal wire shelves along the walls of the freezer.

Bart ran out of the diner and into the deserted street extending through the center of town. He passed more burnt-out cars, ransacked homes, and looted businesses until he reached the parking lot of the small county hospital that was near the next exit to the highway. An ambulance had been overturned and set on fire, and the cars in the parking lot were also burned out. Evening had come upon Cassville, and the only light was from the artificial glow showing from inside the hospital lobby as Bart made his approach.

A number of the florescent tubes used in the ceiling fixtures hadn't been smashed and provided some visibility within the devastated lobby. Bodies of hospital staff and patients had been piled on gurneys and pushed into the open rooms adjoining the lobby area. A faint hissing emanated through the hospital's intercom with the noise of something moving around in the distance being picked up by the system's open mic.

Bart didn't want to risk staying inside the hospital. He thought, "I need to find a vehicle somewhere to drive away and make it to the city. The delivery trucks out in back might still be in one piece. It's worth a shot."

Bart strode out into the dark and onto the lush, well-maintained lawn surrounding the hospital building. A chorus of summertime crickets could be heard, but the environs around the hospital otherwise seemed devoid of life. Several more bodies of patients or staff that had been hurled from the hospital upper levels' many broken windows dotted his path to the loading area in the back of the building.

A body that had been crushed by the force of its impact was dressed in cerulean colored medical scrubs and was lying face down. An ID badge was a few feet from the body's resting place and read, "Douglas Vuković, Resident Practitioner." Bart continued to walk, weaving around the deceased, and then saw the corrugated iron platform of the hospital's loading area.

The loading area's garage door was locked and must have remained so during the chaos at the hospital. An empty truck trailer without a diesel cab was positioned on stilts, blocking the employee parking spaces that were allotted to this area. Bart turned the corner of the truck trailer and saw that one standard-sized delivery truck was parked by itself.

Bart hurried to the driver's side door and saw that it was unlocked. He quickly opened the truck's door and jumped into the driver's seat, closing the door behind him. The truck's cab was unlit, but Bart was able to find a small flashlight in the glove compartment.

Bart had hotwired trucks on the farm, so he hoped that he would be able to do the same with the delivery truck. The glove compartment was still open, so Bart shone the flashlight into its space. A utility knife was in a plastic pouch, and he grabbed it to use as a tool.

The plastic cover on the steering column was wedged tightly in place, but Bart was able to pry it loose with the knife after removing the screws. The bundle of wires fell from the access panel into the barely visible space below the steering wheel.

Bart placed the flashlight handle between his teeth and aimed its light into the panel with the hanging, colored wires. He traced the wires with the color that he concluded indicated ignition and battery, from the experience he had working on older trucks, and found they led straight up into the steering column. Bart stripped the insulation from two of the wires and twisted them together.

The interior lights came on with a jolt, and Bart dropped the flashlight from his mouth into his hand. He found the starter wire and stripped some of the insulation off its end. Bart touched the live end to the battery wires, and the truck engine revved slightly. He put pressure on the gas pedal, and this time the truck revved loudly, settling into a steady rhythm as the engine continued to pump.

There were no lights visible from the truck's cab with minimal illumination from a clouded moon. Bart could see nothing around him, so he turned on the truck's headlights. The headlights flashed on and lit up the concrete divider between the parking space and the line of trees planted in a row near the hospital's outer lawn. Bart heard a keening sound somewhere off in the distance.

The steering column was locked, so Bart searched for the keyhole near the wheel and popped the spring with his knife, breaking the lock. The keening sound was growing louder and was originating from the direction behind the truck.

Bart put the truck into reverse and immediately slammed into something weighty that was not visible from the rearview mirror. He put the truck into drive and spun it around, now facing the loading area of the hospital from where he had found the parking spaces.

There was a crowd of several dozen people running rapidly toward him over the hospital grounds. The keening sound had become saturated and was drowning out the sound of the truck motor as the crowd reached the loading area.

As Bart drove forward to reach the roadway in front of the hospital, a figure sprang from the darkness outside the driver's side window and attempted to pull open the door of the moving vehicle. It was a young woman, whose long hair was partially ripped from its roots, her face streamed with blood; she was snarling and yanking at the door to Bart's compartment. The girl's teeth had been filed into sharp points with an implement.

The girl let out the unnatural, ear-splitting keening that Bart had first heard at the farm and ran alongside the truck as Bart made his escape. She hung onto the driver's side door and took out a large knife with her free hand.

Bart accelerated and attempted to lose her as he barely missed the throng of enraged townspeople wielding axes and bats. Bart heard bodies hit the back of the truck, and the young woman fell off, rolling onto the lawn along the hospital's walkway. The truck was now speeding over the main road through Cassville and then onto the highway leading out of town, its large back compartment shifting and rattling as Bart drove up the exit ramp away from his attackers and into the desolate night.

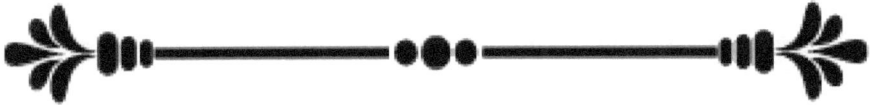

The four-lane highway was flanked by rows of deciduous trees in full summer bloom on either side as Bart drove through the countryside. The night was almost entirely dark with negligible moonlight and a dearth of cars on the road. The chugging of the engine and the wheels turning over asphalt were the only sounds Bart could perceive as the truck's headlights pierced the almost impenetrable blackness before him.

Bart thought about reaching the city, but he considered that it would also be overrun, not knowing how far the insanity had spread. What could have caused this to happen? Has everyone become possessed? "Why haven't I been overtaken by whatever is causing this plague? That buzzing I heard earlier..." Bart hoped to find other survivors, but so far everyone had either become a killer or a victim, besides himself.

Bart flipped on the truck radio and cruised through the AM dials. There was a good deal of static, but Bart was able to find a local news station. The announcer was reading from a statement.

"They are advising everyone to remain in their homes and not to attempt to leave. The Air National Guard will announce when evacuees can be transported to a secure facility. In the meantime, please remain in your homes."

The truck drove slowly up a steep hill and then reached its top. As it made the descent down the hill, the beams of another vehicle's headlights came into view. Bart braced himself and hoped that this was a sign that the city or another nearby town had escaped whatever had infested Cassville and his family's farm.

"No urban center is safe at this time. If you are presently outdoors in an urban center, you are advised to move to another location and seek fortified shelter immediately."

The vehicle's high beams became more intense as they approached Bart's truck, which was moving at a constant pace. The vehicle's occupants were driving at a tremendous rate and passed Bart's truck on the opposite side of the highway almost as if it were standing still. Bart could hear its wheels screech to a halt far behind him and then the sound of the vehicle barreling forward again.

"There are widespread reports of cannibal..." Bart turned the radio knob off and gripped his steering wheel for what appeared would be a fast-moving assault.

Bart could now see from his side-view mirror that the vehicle was a pickup truck. As the pickup truck approached, its high beams shone brightly, making it difficult to see any passengers. Bart tried to accelerate his aging white delivery vehicle with its heavy payload, but he was effectively a slow-moving target on the highway as the truck decelerated and pulled along the driver's side flank.

The reflection of both vehicles' headlights revealed that the truck was festooned with dismembered human limbs and heads strung over its front hood with rope, and graffiti spray painted over the entirety of its outer body. Bart couldn't see the drivers in the truck's cab from his higher position, but the truck's cargo bed held a half dozen crazed occupants armed with axes and baseball bats.

As their truck kept pace with Bart's vehicle, one of the men seated in the cargo bed climbed to the top of the truck's cab roof and supported himself as the two trucks continued down the highway. He stared menacingly at Bart from his perch and put a large hunting knife between his teeth to free his hands. Bart could see that the man's face had been heavily scarred with sharp objects, almost in a ritual fashion, as well as exhibiting the telltale bloodstained tear streaks he had noted on the girl at the hospital and on his family.

The man was posed to leap, when Bart suddenly hit the delivery truck's breaks and receded behind the still-moving pickup truck. The armed man fell into empty space and bounced off the highway's pavement, flopping into a ditch by the roadside.

The pickup truck was not moving as swiftly as it was when it first approached, so the drivers easily swung their vehicle around and came directly at Bart's truck, which was now stationary on the highway. The length of the delivery truck was perpendicular to the four-lane divide, and its back compartment was exposed to the oncoming transport and its crew.

The pickup truck careened into the side of the delivery truck and spun it off the highway from the tremendous force of its impact. Bart was buckled into his seat but his chest slammed into the steering wheel as his truck spun again and again until it hit the tree line off the highway. He was only partially conscious when he heard a deafening explosion and saw the glare of flames in his driver's side mirror.

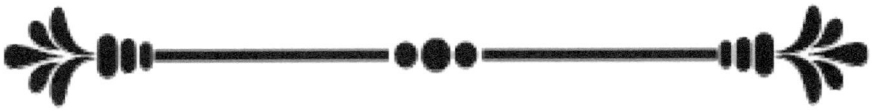

The shattered windshield let in the morning sun, and Bart carefully sat up in the driver's seat. Bart felt his face and chest, examining himself for any obvious signs of trauma. His thick curly black hair held flecks of glass from the accident, which he brushed out with a hand while closing his eyes. The cab's rearview mirror showed no cuts or bruises on him, and he could feel his legs, so Bart unbuckled his seat belt and opened the delivery truck's driver-side door.

The air was acrid with burning gasoline, twisted metal, and blasted corpses. Bart stood beside the delivery truck, facing the highway from last night. The now blackened pickup truck rested in the middle of the highway, still smoldering. The desiccated assailants lay strewn around the finished hull of their means of attack, victims of the broken fuel line that resulted from their collision.

Bart walked around to the other side of the delivery truck and saw that the back compartment had an enormous crater in its center. One of the truck's back wheels was missing, and his means of transportation was otherwise out of commission. Bart lowered his head, rubbing his stiff neck, and contemplated his next action.

"Put your hands in the air where I can see them. Right now!" Bart heard a woman's voice behind him. He gulped and put his hands up over his head, showing that he was weaponless.

"Now turn around, be slow, and let us see your face." Bart did an about face and saw two young women, one holding a single barrel shotgun that was pointed at his head from several yards away.

The unarmed woman spoke up. "He doesn't have the marks. He looks clean."

The woman leveling the shotgun at Bart interjected, "What's your name? Say something!"

"Bartholomew." Bart let his parched mouth hang open. He saw that the women were dressed in blue jeans and T-shirts and did not seem deranged as all the others had been. The fact they had not attacked him instantly was more proof in Bart's mind that they were sane and might help him survive.

"Lisa, search this boy for weapons." Both women were in their twenties, but Lisa was probably the younger one. She walked forward, scrutinized Bart's features, and began searching his shorts pockets. Other than sneakers, Bart was only wearing athletic shorts and a thin T-shirt, so there weren't many places to hide a knife or a gun. The girl ran her hands over his chest and back and then stepped backward, still watching Bart.

"He's got nothing. Looks like you slept in those clothes. Where are you coming from?"

"Outside Cassville. The whole town has been destroyed. Is this everywhere? Can you tell me about the madmen?" Bart kept his hands up and hoped there was a way out.

"It's everywhere. The radio says that all the cities have been overrun. We can't get a TV station anymore. You can put down your arms now."

Bart lowered his arms and put them slack at his sides.

"This is Lisa, as you heard, and I'm Emily. We're sisters, and we're all that's left of our family. We need to get off the road and to the house before someone sees us."

Emily then got behind Bart with her shotgun in both hands and motioned for him to move forward, gesturing with the barrel. Bart followed Lisa, and the three of them stepped off the highway and into a forested area that extended into the hills.

"We heard the explosion last night and thought we should come down here in the morning just in case. You must be the only survivor then."

"Those men in the pickup were insane. They collided with me, and I was pushed off the highway." Bart turned back to look at Emily and motioned with his right hand. "They rammed my truck, but it ended up killing them."

"Yep, they were insane all right. Almost everyone is now. You are the first we've seen who hasn't turned."

They continued along what was now a dirt path running through the woods. A two-story Victorian-style house was up the hill where the trail ended.

"We're up here. We're connected to the highway by a road that only runs past us and then finishes at a dead end. We have to keep the lights off at night so we aren't visible from the highway."

Bart stepped into the thicket and pulled himself up by the young branch of one of the downward-sloping trees. It was a short climb over the hill and into the fenced backyard of the house. Lisa opened the gate and let them into the enclosed yard.

"We lock this up at night too. We've boarded up the windows on both floors from the inside. It's not a fortress, so we might have to barricade ourselves in the basement if things get rough enough."

Bart observed that the yard had a freshly dug mound about ten feet long near its shed. As the two girls and Bart walked onto the house's back porch and opened the door leading inside, Bart could see that chunks of the porch's wooden columns had been blown away with a firearm.

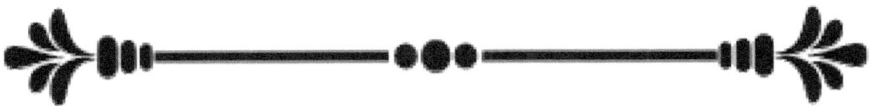

Thin rays of sunlight penetrated the gaps between the boards covering the picture window to the living room. Emily sat down on an upholstered sofa and put the shotgun across her denim-swaddled legs. Bart stood and accepted a glass of water from Lisa, which he guzzled down.

"I could use another one...or two. Where is the kitchen?"

Lisa led Bart to the kitchen lined with cardboard boxes along its single wall, and he drank deeply from the faucet. "I don't have to remember my manners if this is the end of the world." Bart tried to smile at Lisa, but she just watched him wipe his mouth.

Emily turned on the handheld radio that was sitting on the end table next to her sofa. The sound was muted, but Bart could hear it from the kitchen.

"The military has begun burning bodies in mass graves. The Center for Disease Control doesn't know why this is happening or where its source might originate. They are taking no chances, as..."

Emily turned the radio volume down as Bart and Lisa sat across from her on another living room sofa. "What happened to your family? Did they all turn?"

"Yes, my mother and sister tried to murder me right after my grandma tried to do the same. I ran to Cassville and saw what had become of the people there. A mob almost surrounded me, and I drove away when I got into the fight on the road."

Lisa turned to Bart and leaned in. "Have you heard the buzzing yet?" Lisa's face gave away no emotion but Bart could tell that she was clearly agitated when asking the question.

Bart was startled and looked at both of them, saying, "You've heard it too? I felt like I was splitting in half, and then it just ended."

Lisa got up from her resting place on their sofa and walked over to sit next to Emily. They both stared at Bart and were silent for a few moments.

"We were eating breakfast when the buzzing started. Emily and I were in the kitchen and collapsed from the pain. The buzzing seems to be out of this world—it's no earthly sound at all."

"Like you, the buzzing ended for us, and we could stand again. I went to the back door to find our parents and stood right there." Emily pointed at the braided throw rug in the entranceway. "I looked through the side window, and saw our mom and dad eating our younger brother in that yard. They had cut his head off with a shovel and were tearing at his bare arms with their teeth."

Lisa stood up and turned away so Bart couldn't see her expression. Emily continued. "I ran upstairs and grabbed our dad's pump shotgun out of the bedroom closet where he kept it. They were finishing the legs when I threw open the door and started firing. I was able to bring both of them down without reloading. I hit the porch a few times. All three are buried out back."

"Why do you think we didn't go mad? The buzzing must be what changes everyone. I bled from my right eye after the buzzing, and all the crazies have blood marks all over their faces—their own blood."

"We don't know. The buzzing is like a wave washing over a shore and then receding. Once someone is trapped, and they aren't swallowed up, it passes over them. The radio has mentioned the buzzing, but there are some who haven't heard it yet."

Bart, Lisa, and Emily remained huddled around the tiny radio and listened as the signal faded in and out. Reports came in over the course of the day that indicated the military was losing ground and had to fall back, as so many bases and camps had been compromised. The radio-station announcer at one point mentioned that he had barricaded himself inside the station building.

"The streets outside are filling with throngs of butchers, parading their ghastly trophies. I am not sure how long I can continue this broadcast. An armed guard was planning to arrive to escort us to safety—if anywhere is truly safe—but they never appeared. It is only a matter of time before those below make it up to the fifth floor..."

The evening turned into another moonless night. The battery-powered radio crackled, and Emily hunted through the dial for a viable signal, but some had gone out completely. The sound of a diesel truck driving and then coming to a stop nearby issued from the road outside the sisters' house.

Lisa ran to the front door and looked through the small window in the door frame's apex. Lisa whispered over her shoulder, "It's a trucker with no load on the road outside in front of the house. He's only driving his cab."

The three of them had been sitting in the living room with the lights off, as electricity had stopped working before sunset. Emily had lit some candles that were placed on the floor, away from the windows, but she turned on her flashlight and approached the front door. The diesel truck was parked directly in front of the house with its engine off, but its headlights shone into the woodland blackness surrounding the home's front lawn. The crew cab was silver colored and bore the company name "Ward Trucking" detailed into its driver's side door, which was visible from their hiding spot.

"Lisa, that's Uncle Phil's rig! He is alive, then! We have to go outside and get him in here."

Lisa put her hands over the front doorknob and said, "Wait. How do we know that is Uncle Phil? Some of the crazies might have just gotten his truck and drove it out here. Let's see if he steps out and shows himself first."

Nothing stirred from within the cab while the truck's high beams shone into the ring of sparse trees at the country road's dead end. Lisa and Emily were too far away to determine if someone was even in the cab at all.

"We have to check. I'm bringing the shotgun. Hold the flashlight for me." Lisa took Emily's flashlight as she returned to the living room to fetch the pump-action shotgun. Bart followed Emily to the front door, and they walked outside together to stand on the lawn a few yards away from the cab's sealed and darkened enclosure.

"Phil, is that you? We need to make sure that you're OK." Emily held the shotgun in both hands but pointed its barrel away from the cab. "Phil, open the door if you're all right."

The door to the truck's cab flung open, and a misshapen man thing spilled out, charging at Emily. Part of its once-human face was deformed so that the right eye had become gigantic and bulbous, and its gaping mouth was filled with sharp, horn-shaped teeth.

The creature let out a hideous croak as it battered an aghast Emily with an elongated, suckered tentacle where its right arm should have been instead. Lisa shrieked and watched Emily drop her shotgun on the ground as she was choked to death by the tendril wrapped around her throat. Bart turned toward the house's front porch to flee but was pulled off his feet by a second tentacle emanating from the monstrosity's torso.

On the living room table, the radio's news broadcast signal ebbed and was gradually replaced by a sinusoidal humming from within an inhuman voice uttered a mantra over and over: "The Great Egg has opened...it has awakened. The Great Egg has opened...it has awakened. The Great Egg has opened...it has awakened."

The Devil's Garden

There was no light in the coffin, and not much more air. Clarence writhed in the tight, confined space as he surfaced suddenly into horrible consciousness. At once, he pulled his leaden arms from his sides and onto his chest and began pressing against the lid of the coffin with the palms of his hands, becoming more frantic with each faltering push. His own jagged, raspy breath was the only sound Clarence could hear over the cracking of his fingernails as they broke into the overhead enclosure of his buried prison.

Splinters of pine fell onto his parched mouth and forehead, threatening to slip into his eyes. Searing pain bit into him as his fingertips shredded against the wood, with thin streams of blood running over his hands and onto his face. Despite the total blackness of the coffin, Clarence sensed his vision was clouding with each halting, panicked breath. How much time did he have left?

There were muffled noises above him. The garbled intonation of men speaking and then a commotion of vigorous, hurried digging. Clarence paused and lay still, trying to preserve his last remaining breaths. As he drifted into unconsciousness, a shovelhead broke through the wood coffin lid, and a flood of humid, tropical air rushed over him . . .

The window of his fourth-floor hotel room was unlatched and open, offering Clarence a late-night view of the city and its port.

At once, he sprang up in bed, crying out. Nothing—there was nothing. It had just been a dream. He exhaled, perched on the edge of the mattress, and sucked in a deep, deliberate breath. The sheets were damp with sweat, the night's moist air hanging over him.

The nightmare had returned, and so soon after the last one. Each time, Clarence dreamed of being buried alive and then dug up by some unknown interlopers. Yet it was the immediacy of this most recent burial ordeal that surprised him; his passenger ship had docked on the island only this past morning, and this frightful vision of vivisepulture had invaded his dreams the very same night.

The recurring nightmare had been with Clarence since he'd first landed on this ill-fated island several years prior, but tonight's episode had been the most vivid yet. He always got a sense that the burial was occurring somewhere on the island itself, but so little could be grasped from the dream—there was just a dark coffin, his terror at being buried alive, and the men breaking in with a shovel just before he awoke.

Clarence poured tepid water from the pitcher on the worn table across from his bed. He refilled the pitcher and washed his stubbled face before drying himself with a rough cloth. The ceramic toilet set and the ornately carved table had seen better days, but still retained some of their original colonial elegance. Few visitors came to this island, but those who did most often sought their fortunes—even at the risk of their lives.

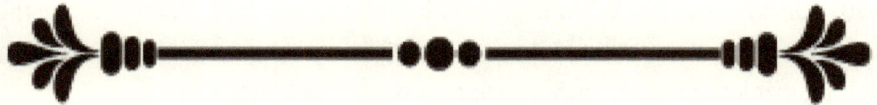

The early morning bustle on the street outside the hotel stirred Clarence from the shallow, fitful sleep he'd found after waking from the nightmare. He was to meet a man at *Café la Plantation* to discuss the shipping of contraband goods off the island. The coastal city on the other side of the calm, green-blue sea was the goods' destination.

The island was a haven for sellers of illicit cargo, possessing little in the way of effective government and even less in the way of law enforcement. The last of the occupying foreign soldiers were leaving the island for good and, in their absence, a void of any unifying authority.

Clarence stood in front of the oval floor mirror resting on an upright frame near the room's door. He'd not bothered shaving, and had dressed in a white summer suit and straw boater hat. He adjusted a silk necktie under his pressed shirt collar.

The faint dark circles under his eyes betrayed Clarence's sleeplessness, but he hoped Junior wouldn't notice. He and Junior had done business on several occasions, and it was Clarence's heartfelt wish this would be the last time he would make the journey to the island.

The handful of runs Junior had conducted with Clarence had always been from the eastern part of the island, which was a separate, autonomous nation unto itself. If the pending deal with Junior was closed, it would set Clarence up in relative comfort, and he could abandon the smuggling life for some less risky line of work.

The mirror's glass was very polished, in sharp contrast to the otherwise dingy hotel room. This cheval mirror might have even been lifted at some point from one of the many ruined plantations in the island's interior.

Giving himself one final glance over, Clarence reached out to touch the glass. His reflection distorted as the mirror began to tilt upward. He looked down as it pivoted toward him and saw his reflection, now a mass of liquescent flesh, tumorous and suppurating, crawling with turgid maggots.

Clarence grasped the border of the mirror and held it tightly, staring into the silvery glass. The horror was gone; his face's reflection was finely wrinkled and weathered but hale, as it had been only a moment before.

A chill came over Clarence as he thought on the repulsive visage. "Nerves, that's all it was," Clarence assured himself, "bad dreams are chasing me even into daytime. A shot of vermouth at *Café la Plantation* will do me good."

The street outside the hotel was filled with vendors, men pushing produce carts, and women carrying baskets on their heads. The scent of ripe fruit mixed with the foul air of the city washed over Clarence as he stepped out, the fetid aroma accentuated by the humid climate. *Café la Plantation* was but a few city blocks over from the hotel.

"In dollars, not francs, like you asked." Clarence placed the dull brown paper envelope on the café table and grabbed a peeling wooden chair from nearby, seating himself across from Junior.

"And good day to you as well, Clarence. Where are your manners?" Junior said in heavily accented English. He smiled broadly, quickly reaching across the table and stuffing the envelope into his pants pocket, glancing around the café as he did so.

Clarence replied, "*Bonjour, Monsieur* Junior. You look well. The molasses trade must have been good to you of late, especially now prohibition is done."

Junior wrinkled his forehead and leaned into the table. "*Monsieur* Clarence, I have to say, I'm surprised to see you back. Maybe the money was just too good to pass up, no?"

Clarence recalled his first meeting with Junior and the dangerous runs they had completed together: moving alcohol and sugarcane molasses to the mainland at great risk to their safety and the lives of their crew. Junior had guts, but Clarence had never fully learned to trust him, and now was no exception.

Junior had been born and raised on the island but had learned English from "your army men and a missionary schoolteacher." He was a young man, vigorous and self-assured, but always cloaked in uncertainty; Junior was a wild card even among the tumultuous environs of the island. Clarence still did not even know Junior's given name, as he had never revealed it.

Clarence looked directly at Junior. "Like you, I'm getting squeezed by the new laws on booze. Why would someone buy from us when it's now legal and on the shelves again? But we can still undercut the competition on molasses; no tariffs, no taxes, so lower prices for our customers. This is a buy I can't pass up."

A waiter came to their table and Clarence ordered a shot of vermouth.

Junior waited for the waiter to leave before leaning back in his seat and grinning. "We'll meet tonight at the docks not far from here and take an old tug up the coast. The loading place is in a jungle spot I've used before, where no one will look for us. The streets will be empty—this is the first night of the Feast of Souls. Everyone will be inside their homes or at the cemeteries, so you don't have to worry about being followed.

"The whole cargo will be placed on your sea-worthy ship and, from there, you can take it back home. Your crew will be on that ship, *Monsieur* Clarence?"

Clarence nodded, trying to keep his face unreadable. "They were paid in part before I left and will be there. Just a skeleton crew—after all, we want to involve as few as possible. I'm much more careful now than I was in the past. Your people will supply the labor to load the goods, I take it?"

Junior's face twitched, but before he could speak, the waiter returned. He took a crystal shot glass from his tray and placed it in front of Clarence before turning and departing.

"Yes, *Monsieur* Clarence," Junior said, his composure restored, "you don't worry about that. Our men will never breathe a word, I promise you. See you at nine o'clock."

Clarence walked back to his hotel, feeling a bit lighter now that the first part of his last trip was done. The taste of the vermouth lingered in his mouth, and now he needed some breakfast. The hotel had a small dining room where he could get a plate of eggs with plantains. The late morning and afternoon would provide the time for Clarence to read the sale papers he had brought with him and plot out what would happen to this sizable shipment once he was back in port.

The morning and afternoon passed quickly. Clarence spent the time working at the table in his room and had lunch brought up to him from the hotel kitchen. Papers were spread over the makeshift desk, with his open leather journal displaying the figures he had calculated and jotted down. Junior had received the advance payment, and the rest would be paid to the smuggling crew's captain once Clarence took possession of his cargo.

He finished what was left of his lunch for supper and then prepared to go down to the docks to meet Junior. The late autumn sun was beginning to set over the horizon and rosy-fleeced light spilled in through the open window of his hotel room. Clarence sat on his bed and looked out over the city and to the sea beyond it, knowing it would soon be dark. The streets would be deserted, just as Junior had said— tonight was the first night of the festival.

"Will you be back soon, *Mesye*?" The woman at the hotel's front desk said as Clarence walked by her station. "Tonight's not a good night to be out on those streets, especially for a Yankee. Why don't you just get some sleep instead?"

Clarence could see the young woman was genuinely concerned, so he stopped and shot her a reassuring smile. "A friend told me there's a festival tonight, a feast for the dead. I'd heard about it during other visits, but I was never here when the festival took place. People were always reluctant to speak of what went on. I'm eager to see what all the fuss is about."

From here, the streets outside appeared pitch black, with no signs of lights from other buildings or passersby. The weather had cooled, a balmy breeze wafting through the hotel's yellow-painted double doors and over Clarence and the young woman. She leaned forward from the check-in counter, her long, curly, reddish hair loose, spilling down her heavily freckled face. Her expression was now quite anxious.

"You are right, *Mesye*. It is the *Fet Gede*, the night when the world of the dead and the world of the living are closest. During the day, the people were in the streets, but now they are seeing their families who have passed on. But who knows who is out there? I tell you, it's not safe."

"Restless spirits?" Clarence was just about able to hide his amusement. "I'm just meeting someone. I'll stick to the main thoroughfare as a precaution. But thanks for your concern; I appreciate it."

Despairing, the woman breathed in a hoarse whisper, "It's the *Culte des Mortes*, *Mesye. Jaden Dyab la a*. The Devil's Garden. Stay away from the graveyards this night and the next, no matter who invites you there. I will pray that *les Saints Bénis* keep you."

Clarence gave her a final confused smile before turning and sauntering out onto the empty street of the hotel district. The woman watched him go, her sad eyes boring into his back until, at last, the darkness swallowed him.

The hard-packed dirt streets of the city were ill-maintained, but an extensive tram system ran through the downtown area and its adjacent districts, which belied the abject poverty of the capital and of the island itself. The public trams had ceased running several hours ago, and Clarence proceeded on foot to his appointment with Junior.

Single lights, probably candles, flickered in the open windows of tenement homes, but otherwise, the streets were sheltered in darkness. The moon was only a waning crescent but provided most of the remaining illumination from its perch in the cloudy night sky. In the distance, Clarence spied a long procession of lights advancing in single-file out of the city, but he was too far away to make out any more than that.

Turning a street corner, Clarence was nearing his destination. The waterfront had recently undergone new construction, and a concrete wharf had been added, which extended ahead of the antiquated wooden docks built during the city's founding. As he paused in front of a dilapidated shipwright's warehouse near the open avenue, a shadow cast itself over him, seemingly from nowhere.

Clarence looked around and saw nothing. The street was quiet and empty. He took out a packet of *Gaulois Bleu* from his coat's front pocket and lit one with his silver lighter, taking a long drag before continuing on. Only moments later, he paused again, a shadow casting itself into his path, this time from behind. It was larger now, and it had a shape: the shape of a man.

Clarence turned and again saw nothing. Did someone know about his meeting with Junior? Perhaps a rival smuggler? Clarence never carried a weapon—he had always feared arrest more than robbers—but now, and not for the first time, he regretted being without a gun.

Spinning back around, he hurried on, pulling his jacket tight around him despite the warm evening. The nighttime sea stretched out to his right, its cresting waves glimmering in the faint moonlight, and he traced a route along the edge of the water by the docks. The docks were destitute, the cluster of ships parked in the city's harbor without occupants. If someone was planning on attempting to waylay him, he would have to make a run for the hotel, which was now blocks away.

There was someone in the distance. A figure stood near a tugboat moored to the dock, their features not yet visible in the dim light. The boat bobbed slightly in the warm sea wind, and Clarence hurried his step. An enormous shadow spread itself across his path as he moved, the outline of the figure's top hat and long-sleeved coat now clear. Clarence froze and stared at the animated silhouette which abruptly gestured to him, tipping its hat and then waving a hand in a gesture of farewell.

The shadow receded behind a stack of shipping crates and barrels, slowly retreating from Clarence's view. When he looked up, he found Junior walking toward him.

"*Monsieur* Clarence, what is that expression on your face? You see your dead papa or something?" Junior's smirk was obvious even in the low light.

"I . . . I just saw a man. I think he was following me." Clarence felt uneasy, steadying himself as he tossed his spent cigarette butt into the gently churning waves splashing up against the mooring poles.

"There is no man, Clarence. No one is here. Just us and the souls of the dead who roam this night. Let's get on the boat; the crew is waiting."

Clarence quickly scanned the docks before following Junior down the boarding ramp and onto the tugboat. The boat's captain was behind the tug's helm, but none of the other crewmen showed themselves.

Junior unmoored the tug from the docks, throwing the length of rope back onto the ramp as the captain nodded and started the boat's engine. The engine sputtered and convulsed for a moment before chugging along at an even pace. At last, the tug drifted away from the docks and out to sea, gaining speed as the harbor grew smaller. Once they were past the city's limits, they made a hard turn toward the shore.

The tugboat parted the murky waters, white-capped frothing waves breaking from its port and starboard sides. The tug's destination was a remote and mostly uncharted jungle clearing near the island's sparsely populated interior.

The night sky had become clear, and Clarence stood at the tugboat's bow, gazing up into the starry canopy above him, nearly lost in thought. He heard Junior say something to the captain from the bridge behind him, but the chugging of the tug's engine drowned out the words.

"There are no excuses! You men are just lazy rats."

The four crew members stared up at Clarence sullenly as he berated them.

"We're behind schedule now, because of this." Clarence stood in front of the men as the sun began to set over the sea behind him, looking down at them from the chartered merchant ship's main hatch. Clarence had hired the ship and its crew to transport this run of illicit goods from the island, but the ship's captain wasn't entirely clear on the nature of the cargo.

Normally a very silent man, the ship's first mate spoke up. "We only did as you asked us. You were wrong about how long loading the ship would take. There was more cargo than what was written on the shipper's ledger." The first mate was an experienced seaman—taciturn, rough, and haggard—but was articulate in his own way.

Clarence sighed, his anger dissipating. "I went by what the suppliers' estimate. Now let's get this finished and be on our way. I'm losing money as we bicker over this mess." Clarence stepped down and walked away, ignoring the glare the first mate gave him as he descended the ship's stairs to his quarters below deck.

This was not the first time Clarence had spoken harshly to the crew; he and the captain had maintained a working relationship that had lasted several years. Clarence had cultivated a reputation for callousness, even cruelty, among the captain's sailors, and the men had quickly grown to resent him. This commercial ship had run most of his biggest jobs from the island during prohibition.

The chartered ship would leave port that evening on a voyage due to last almost a week. The trip would end with a late-night docking in the waters outside the discharge port. The cargo would then be transported to shore on smaller, more nimble vessels so the goods could evade customs. Clarence wasn't sure if the ship's crew knew the value of the cargo they were carrying, but the ship's captain was a long-time retainer, and Clarence believed he could be trusted.

There was a knock at the cabin door. "Clarence, may I have a word with you?" It was the gruff voice of the ship's captain.

"Please, come in," Clarence replied without rising from his desk.

The door opened and the captain entered, his bearded face shadowy in the low light of the Bakelite desk lamp. "The men are becoming angry and frustrated," the captain announced. "First Mate Dorman came to me and said they are being overworked. That you are pushing them too hard to make an impossible schedule." The captain was an older man who'd spent many years at sea, and often left Clarence to supervise the crew while they loaded and unloaded his goods.

"Not true at all, Captain Hancock," was Clarence's measured response. "It's the men's fault we're behind as they didn't follow the schedule. If we're late to the offshore meet-up point, the handlers won't be there with the boats. No boats, no way to get the cargo to shore. We'd have to turn around and go back out to sea."

41

Captain Hancock stepped back and seemed to be weighing something up in his head. Clarence knew he was a valuable client and that the captain knew a serious disagreement with him might very well lead to his business being taken elsewhere. "I'll see what I can do with the men. You're right—we can't miss the drop-off point or it will cost us all."

The captain tipped his peaked cap to Clarence and then slowly closed the cabin door. The muffled sound of the captain's footsteps echoed from the stairwell and then, for a few moments, from the deck above. Clarence sat and stared at the closed door as the footsteps faded, returning to the task at hand only once they were gone.

With his bookkeeping ledgers open in front of him, Clarence noted with satisfaction that this shipment of rum, molasses, and spices would be his most lucrative yet. The final sale of these goods would elevate Clarence's smuggling business into a new class of operation. He would no longer need to retain Captain Hancock with his aging watercraft and surly crew; he would be able to afford a ship of his own and his own men. Clarence wondered with some amusement whether Captain Hancock's crew were tempted to mutiny, given how large a sum of money was involved in this transaction. Did Hancock's men understand the full worth of what was being shipped?

The sound of footsteps and a hurried knock abruptly broke Clarence's stream of thought. A voice spoke from the other side of the cabin door: "We are docking to refuel, Mr. Morris. Please come above deck in fifteen minutes."

Clarence stood and rushed to open the door. A young man—a member of the crew—stood in front of him.

"Fifteen minutes, sir. We need to stop before going out to sea."

Clarence gripped the edge of the open door in frustration. He sputtered angrily, "There was no scheduled stop. Who approved this?"

The crewman replied, "First Mate Dorman, sir. We didn't have time to refuel due to all hands on the loading dock, so we are stopping now."

Slamming the door without a word, Clarence returned to his desk. He gathered his business papers and put them into the desk's top drawer, locking the drawer with the small key he kept on a chain around his neck. Clarence glanced at his reflection in the cabin's framed wall mirror and placed his straw boater hat on his head. As he turned his back on the mirror to leave, a caliginous shape, darkling and nebulous, began to form within the mirror's surface.

The ship had made slow progress along the island's coast and was now far from a port of any size. Clarence stood on the upper deck and gazed out at the sea, its waves sparkling in the bright moonlight of the evening. Their modestly sized steamship was headed toward a set of wooden piers, exhaust smoke trailing from its twin funnels. The piers protruded into the shallow waters of the jungle's shoreline; standing atop them were several men who appeared to be waiting for them.

The ship docked, and the men began moving barrels from the adjacent pier to the ship: fuel for the oil-fired steam boilers. Clarence saw that Captain Hancock and First Mate Dorman were already on the shore, moving between tents pitched in the clearing and speaking with some of the local men. Clarence walked up the two makeshift planks connecting the ship to the pier and sought out the clump of tents nestled at the fore of the jungle's tangled undergrowth.

"Come sit with us, Clarence. Armand here is going to share some of his spiced rum." Captain Hancock was in a jovial mood; he seemed a different man to the old captain who'd questioned Clarence earlier. Clarence seated himself on one of the folding canvas chairs in front of the camp's main tent, between the captain and first mate.

The captain placed a coarse hand on Clarence's shoulder, reassuring him. "Our ship should be ready within the hour, and you can get some rest after a nightcap. Here, drink up." The young man Captain Hancock had introduced as Armand handed Clarence a drink in a glass tumbler.

"Thanks," offered Clarence as he took his first shallow sip from the green enameled tumbler. Strong stuff—the spice was almost cloying to Clarence's palate.

Clarence studied the campsite beyond the open fire, the only source of light nearby besides the oil lamps that hung from posts dotting the camp. Some of the laborers were standing nearby, restless and shifty. Clarence took another drink from the tumbler, noting Captain Hancock was holding an empty glass.

"Mr. Morris, you seem sleepy. Why don't you finish your rum and then head to the ship? We'll be embarking soon." First Mate Dorman hovered near Clarence's chair. His voice was acerbic, almost mocking in tone, his timeworn features hollow in the light of the flickering flames.

Clarence put the tumbler to his lips, but it fell from his hand, the remaining rum spilling out over his clothes. He tried to stand but felt dizzy, dropping back onto the flimsy chair behind him. Slowly, he slid onto the sandy ground.

43

He felt hands take hold of his deadened limbs, lifting him up . . .

But what happened next? Clarence looked away from the tugboat's bow and up into the late-night sky again, as if waking from a trance. Junior called to him: "*Monsieur* Clarence, the captain wishes to have a word with you."

The times that followed that night at the camp had not been good ones. Clarence never recovered his cargo, which set him back years financially. His succeeding memory was of wandering along a deserted beach in the early morning, his mouth and skin parched, his white suit soiled and torn.

Clarence had found his way from the beach to a small town several miles away and hitched a ride on a cart back to the city. Days had passed unaccounted for. Accepting a loan from a business associate, Clarence purchased a ticket on a steamer headed home. He never saw Captain Hancock or his crew again.

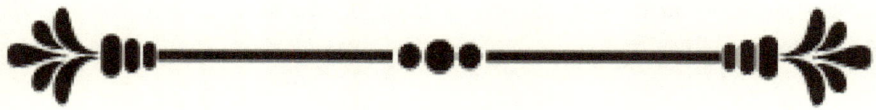

The isolated cove consisted of a natural clearing in the jungle, a white sandy beach, and a single but sturdy pier lit by hanging lanterns extending out into the littoral waters. The tugboat docked, and Junior roped it securely to its moorings. Clarence stepped from the creaky deck onto the pier from a raised plank and peered around. The sandy beach was empty, but a trail led off into the jungle from which flickering lights were visible.

Clarence hadn't seen anyone else on the tug besides Junior and the tug's captain. Also, where were his hired ship and its crew?

Turning, Clarence saw Junior disappearing down the trail and into the jungle. The outline of his moving form was barely visible against the shelter of the tree ferns and tall hardwoods lining the pathway. Clarence stepped onto the stretch of fine sand in front of him, crossing the threshold from the shore to the jungle clearing, and then stepped onto the trail, following Junior.

The tropical forest around him was very active, humming with the ambient nighttime sounds of insect life. Clarence stopped to remove his boater hat and wipe the accumulated sweat from this brow. Where was Junior? He could no longer see him up ahead.

He emerged onto another clearing surrounded by jungle, lit only by a small bonfire at its center. As Clarence approached, erratic shadows danced in the grass, and large, exaggerated shapes loomed amid the trees.

Clarence saw a line of ragged men lifting crates and barrels onto a series of rolling flatbed carts, the carts having been perhaps retrieved from some derelict railway station. The men's actions were stiff and awkward, their steps mechanical and halting. As Clarence drew closer, he could see all of them were very gaunt, with sunken eyes and ashen complexions.

There was a rustling noise from among the ferns close to the trail. From behind Clarence, another of the gaunt men trod out of the jungle, his pallid face impassive and unblinking. Without noticing Clarence, he shambled past him across the clearing and took up the trail's path, which continued at the clearing's far side. The macabre figure was carrying something—it laid across his outstretched arms.

Clarence watched the gaunt man for a brief time before following at a distance behind him. Maybe, he reasoned, the man would lead him to Junior.

The trail snaked through the dense jungle, leading up a shallow hill and then back down again to the jungle floor. Upon descending, Clarence saw the crumbling edifice of a once-stately plantation, its former palatial splendor evident even now.

The gaunt man made his way up the vine-strewn steps of the plantation's columnated exterior and then through its partially open doors, vanishing from view. Clarence paused at the base of the hill and examined the grand building. The broken windows of both floors showed no light within; only the muted illumination of the crescent moon through the jungle canopy revealed any details of the abandoned dwelling.

Clarence hurried across the half-buried cobblestone path to the wide double doors. He pushed inside and paused at the foot of a blighted imperial staircase. Clarence could see the plantation house had indeed been a grand château for its master—gilded portraits hung on every wall, and a ballroom adjacent to the foyer stretched off into shadow. Clarence listened for the sound of footsteps, but none could be heard.

He eased past the cracked rococo doors of the ballroom. In its center stood a strange thing: a large cheval mirror, very similar to the one in his hotel room but much heavier and of more elaborate design. Resting about the mirror were many fetishes and unlit votive candles, black and sickly in color. The mirror was both repulsive and attractive at once, and Clarence was drawn toward it.

"There you are, *Monsieur* Clarence. We've been waiting for you."

Clarence turned sharply to see Junior stepping out of the shadows of the ballroom's interior. His face was painted chalky white, with thick black lines framing his eyes and mouth.

The votive candles surrounding the mirror flared and began burning brightly, revealing the other men who had formed a wide ring around Clarence. The men's faces were painted in the same ritual fashion as Junior's, the make-up resembling a kind of death mask. They stood silently, as if waiting for someone's arrival.

Distant drums began to beat somewhere outside, their rhythms swelling and rising. Clarence eyed the men assembled before him, licking his lips and trying to count them—fifteen maybe, or more. At once, he bolted, barreling past Junior, but two men—God, they were fast—seized him by the arms and dragged him back. They threw him down before the mirror, in which a shape as black as a funeral pall was now forming.

Looking away, Clarence shut his eyes and clasped his ears to shield them from the manic cadence of the rising drums. The sound grew louder, filling the space of the gutted ballroom. Clarence gasped, sweat beading on his skin, his head jerking in a panicked spasm toward the mirror as an enormous shadow cast itself between him and this portal to the world of the dead.

Junior spoke in a clear, powerful voice: "Papa called you back from across the sea, Clarence. That is why you were having those dreams. Your men betrayed you, gave you to Papa to make into one of his servants. You came to your senses once you were pulled out of the ground, and you got away. No one's ever done that before, I'll give you that.

"But now you are here, and Papa will collect what is his on this night, the night when the world of the dead and the world of the living are closest."

Clarence panted and gulped, his terror tightening in his throat. Then, finding the strength to speak, he shouted above the din of the drums, "What is his? What of mine is Papa's?"

Junior smirked and then nodded toward the mirror. "Why, your soul, *Monsieur* Clarence. Papa wants your soul."

A pair of massive arms reached out of the mirror, stygian as the night, and seized Clarence around the waist.

Clarence let out a scream, its sound nearly drowned out by the wildly thrashing drums, his body pulled into the mercury surface of the mirror. He seemed to melt away piece by piece, until only a single straining hand remained, clawing at nothing. Soon, that too disappeared into the netherworld of the mirror.

Far-off cries echoed from somewhere, and at once, the beating drums fell silent. Junior stepped toward the now-dormant mirror, touching his fingers to the glass.

The gaunt men labored near the spent bonfire, having worked throughout the night. Their task was almost done, and rays of morning sunlight were scattered through the giant fronds of the tree ferns sheltering the jungle clearing. The cargo was assembled, loaded onto the flatbed carts; it was almost ready to be pushed across the long trail of wooden planks set back to the beach. A newly arrived commercial steamer was docked at the pier.

Junior stood at the planks' end, where the sandy beach met the pier. He lit a *Gauloises* taken from a packet in his pocket and adjusted the straw boater hat on his head. The steamer's captain walked up the ramp from his ship and raised an arm in greeting.

"Good morning," the captain called out. "What a night it was! We were well ahead of schedule when a terrible storm came out of nowhere." The captain was young but was not a novice seaman. He and his crew had been badly shaken by a ferocious tempest which had beset them the previous night, the likes of which they had never seen before.

Junior flashed a grin. "Strange—we waited for you, but you never came. The sea was peaceful at these shores, like the way I sleep at night." He ambled his way across the planks to join the captain on the pier.

The captain eyed Junior as he approached, frowning slightly. "Even our radio signal was jammed. The waters to these ports are usually so calm, like you said, but we were tossed on the waves for hours. I was sure we were done for when the storm just rolled back, almost as quickly as it had come, exactly at midnight." Removing his seaman's cap for a moment, the captain wiped his brow with a cloth he kept in his trouser pocket, the heat from the island's morning sun already bearing down on him.

Junior held his lit cigarette between two fingers and offered the captain one, which the man accepted. "Mr. Morris had to leave very early this morning," Junior said. "Business matters that couldn't wait another day. We'll load the steamer's hold with his cargo, and you can be on your way."

The captain nodded, took a shaky puff from the *Gauloises*, and, without a word, turned to walk back down the ramp to the deck of his ship. Junior strolled along the planks to the hidden clearing in the jungle and found his older brother, Armand, at work. Armand was herding the ghastly troupe of laborers back into the plantation house where the steamer's crew wouldn't see them. He and Junior would then push the full carts to the pier and help the crew unload the cargo.

"Hey, Bénison, where you get the *blanc* from?" Armand gestured toward one of the gaunt men shuffling near the end of the line. The man had the same withered countenance and vacant, staring eyes as the others, but seemed out of place among the workers. His skin was particularly pale, and he wore a tattered white suit coat which had once clearly been a piece of fine clothing.

Junior replied, "Oh, just someone who owed Papa a debt." He then grinned devilishly. "A debt which has now been repaid."

Cast in Amber

T he young shepherd held his torch high and peered expectantly into the surrounding darkness. He thought he'd heard a noise somewhere in the distance, but now only the deathly silence of the night greeted him. *What was that?* Costa thought, now alarmed. It had seemed like the cry of some animal, but he couldn't be certain.

He turned and slowly walked away from the cliff's sloping ledge. Ahead stretched the subtle trail of footprints left by his father and the hunting party, leading deep into the cave. The band of men had tracked the wolves for several days to what they believed was their lair, but this cave seemed to be something else. What was once a natural cavern had been recast into a kind of hypogeum, with ghastly totems of carnage set on either side of its entrance. *Who could have put such a warning here? Surely not the wolves,* Costa thought as he scrutinized the totems, shivering slightly in the cool nighttime air.

There were sudden cries, as if the men had been startled, their astonished gasps echoing from the cavern below. Costa heard his father as he strode forward to investigate: "Costa, remain on your guard!" A pause. Then: "It's nothing, only a picture on the wall."

Obeying his father without a word, Costa climbed back to the dusty, flat plateau that met the cave's mouth and resumed his watch. He made a final glance at the entrance totems. They were fashioned from human skulls, any flesh long since stripped bare. Shuddering involuntarily, Costa again gazed out into the hushed night and the stark wilderness around him, its mass of tortured oaks and twisted brambles abutting the foot of the cave's barren hill.

Now that he was sure his son was at his station, Rufus returned his attention to the strange mural. Under the light of their torches, he and the other shepherds studied the daubed ochre rendering of a she-wolf suckling her two cubs. The painting was large, sprawling across the wall of the cave. What had shocked Rufus and his men was the strikingly lifelike depiction of the mural's cubs, portrayed as a disturbing mélange of wolf and human child, their eyes feral but keen, their paws almost like hands.

"There is much more to this wolf-pack than we suspected," Rufus said, fear creeping into his voice as he looked over the grim faces at his side. "These are not ordinary wolves, but profane spirits, cursed by the gods for some terrible crime. Stephanus spoke the truth when he said these beasts can assume the form of men."

Stepping away from the wall painting, Rufus pointed onward. "We must be quick. Aurelia may be somewhere in the cave."

The party followed Rufus deeper into the tenebrous passageway, making fleeting glances at the mural as they filed past. As they descended into depths of the cavern, the band's waning torches cast gigantic shadows, exaggerated imitations of the cave's hanging stalactites, protruding rock formations, and the men's own proportions.

From among the villagers Rufus had chosen four men and his elder son for his hunting party. Their steadings had been beset by a pack of roaming wolves and, while the attacks had lasted less than a fortnight, the loss of livestock was all but unbearable. Their village was isolated from the larger towns and cities; the provincial authorities in the distant capital were too far removed to be reached in time. The final attack ended with one shepherd's daughter being carried off by the wolves, taken from her bed as she slept.

Aurelia's father, Caius, unexpectedly halted, stopping the party in its tracks. "Did you hear that?" he said to his fellows, his voice strained and urgent as he choked out the words. "There's a girl sobbing, somewhere ahead. That's my daughter. My Aurelia!"

The men listened, but all that was audible was the distant sound of dripping water monotonously tapping against stone. In a panic, Caius pushed past Rufus and another shepherd, rushing forward into the darkness of the cave, his torch held out before him. Caius fell with a clatter and disappeared, crying out as the light from his torch was abruptly extinguished.

Shouting down into the cave's passage, Rufus exclaimed, "Caius, you fool, you've put us all in danger!" He then scoured the blackness with his torch but failed to see where Caius had fallen. Rufus turned to his men, hastily instructing them: "Go grab him, and then let's search for any sign of Aurelia. Caius couldn't have gotten too far ahead."

Rufus had only taken a few steps before he noticed two sets of glowing red eyes watching the men intently from the cave's gloaming recesses. Under flickering torchlight, the faint outline of an enormous wolf's head appeared, with a second wolf of similar size trailing not far behind it.

The first wolf leaped as Rufus drew his *gladius* from his belt, a relic from his time in the legion. The shepherd before Rufus was taken down with a piercing scream, the massive wolf tearing the man's throat out with one quick laceration from its jaws. Rufus spun, finding several more sets of glinting lupine eyes propagating around him in the shadows.

Rufus thrust with his *gladius*, stabbing deeply into a charging wolf. Howling, the beast fell aside. Rufus dropped his sputtering torch and bolted past its bleeding carcass. Two wolves gave chase, but Rufus's aged yet sturdy legs sped him forward. The dying shrieks of his men rang out from the cavern walls as they were torn to gory shreds, the victims of yet more wolves.

Tumbling out onto the hill's rocky plateau, Rufus nearly stumbled over the mutilated body of his son, the boy's dead eyes staring up into the night's starry heavens. The wolves continued to pursue their quarry, loping down through the brush surrounding the sloping hill and then out into the open fields spanning it, the waving grasses trampled beneath Rufus's sandaled feet.

As he ran, Rufus rapidly scanned the moonlit horizon for somewhere to climb, anywhere the wolves might not reach him. Not far ahead was a hillside cluster of sparsely distributed trees near an outcropping of jutting rocks.

Scaling the trunk of a sagging oak, Rufus pulled himself onto its generous bough and lay, arms clutching the wide branch. He crawled along its length, reaching a spot at its middle, near the craggy cliffs of the hill. Rufus checked his belt and realized he had dropped his *gladius* as he'd fled the caves.

The howls of the wolf pack grew nearer as they closed in on his hillside hiding place. Out the corner of his eye, Rufus spied the shape of a huge wolf perched on a cliff facing his tree branch. The wolf pounced just as Rufus tried to roll away,

51

ripping him from the branches of the oak and onto the ground below. Rufus was silent as he met his death in the slavering jaws of the black wolf, a stoic soldier until the end.

Dragging the mangled corpse of the hunting party's leader behind it, the black-furred wolf returned to its pack. The alpha dropped Rufus's savaged remains onto the cave floor, where it lay surrounded by the gnawed and littered bones of the wolf pack's prey, both man and animal.

The wolf stretched out onto its forepaws before its assembled packmates, almost fluidly metamorphosing into a man. A teenage girl sat before a great gray wolf crouching on its haunches, her plain linen tunic torn and disheveled as she looked on.

The man rose from the cave floor and brought the girl to her bare feet, wrapping her in his sinewy arms in a perverse embrace. At first caressing the girl's neck, his bloody hand came to rest upon her shoulder as he began to speak to his brethren: "Soon, there will be new cubs," the man said, his voice a low and menacing growl. "The pack will swell in number. The usurpers will then know fear, as did our forebearers who were laid to waste before them."

Wild-eyed and filthy, the girl tittered insanely as the pack leader finished his vow, her mind mostly gone. The man turned her to face him, leaning down to meet the girl's parched lips and kissing her deeply on the mouth. The wolf pack howled in unison, a chilling howl of vengeance, their call reverberating off the blood-drenched walls of the wolf den and echoing out into the desolate night.

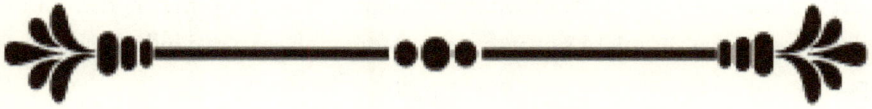

Appius and Lucius sat idly beside each other on a bench in the provincial governor's villa, one of many carved marble benches in the lengthy hallway. They rested in the shade of the villa's columnated front entrance, finding their seat cool to the touch despite the hot day outside.

Stirring for a moment, Lucius peered down the empty hallway. At the end of the row of benches was a statue of the emperor in military dress, the unoccupied space's only guardian. At once both regal and ascendant, the emperor's likeness conveyed a spirit of triumph after many hard-won victories. His uncle, Lucius noticed, was nodding off, but started when a young attendant appeared at his side.

"This way, please. The proconsul will see you now," the attendant said stiffly, walking quickly ahead and not bothering to note whether he was being followed. The travel-weary twosome trudged after the youth, who soon stopped in front of an open archway. "Here. Someone will return for you after your meeting with the proconsul." Unsmiling, the attendant then strode off, failing to make eye contact with either of his charges even once.

Appius glanced over at his nephew as they stood before the archway. "Big city manners," he said, shrugging wryly. Then, gesturing forward, he said, "You lead the way, Lucius. Proconsul Drusus hasn't seen you since you were a child."

Lucius stepped into the proconsul's official chambers, an open, spacious office featuring shelf after shelf of bound scrolls along its brightly painted walls. The arched and glassless windows of the chamber provided a picturesque view of the capital's calm seaside harbor and the azure summer sky under which it was sheltered. A stern-looking older man, robed in the long tunic and *pallium* of his position, turned to greet the visitors as Lucius drew near, Appius at his side.

"So, this is Rufus Norbanus' younger son, Lucius," the man said, at first seeming dispassionate but then breaking into a broad smile, the creases around his eyes stretching to his graying temples. "Come," the proconsul said as he looked over Lucius, "sit here and let's catch up on what the family has been doing out on the estates."

Proconsul Publius Claudius Drusus embraced Appius by clasping both the man's muscular forearms before resting on a reclining couch near his desk, offering the remaining two seats to Appius and Lucius.

"I'm afraid I am the bearer of bad news, Publius Drusus," Appius explained, somber as he braced himself for what was to come. "My brother, Rufus Flaccus, is dead, as is his elder son and my nephew, Costa. They were slain in the pursuit of a girl from our village who had been taken by a pack of wolves. None in the hunting party had returned after more than a week, so we have assumed the worst." Appius studied Publius Drusus's austere, aquiline face, worried that even Rufus's former commander might be shattered after learning about the death of his old friend.

Publius sat in silence as Rufus finished speaking. "Are you sure, Appius?" he said slowly, stunned. "You have nothing but a prolonged absence to confirm their deaths?" Publius had become visibly crestfallen, an abrupt change from his almost buoyant demeanor just moments ago.

"The council of elders debated sending a rescue party, but the howls of the wolves were heard outside the village soon after," Appius replied, feeling a slight chill upon recalling that night's rapacious howling. "If Rufus and his men had found the wolf den, either they would have slain the wolves, or the wolves killed them. The hunter, Quintus, was with the party and he could track a beast to the ends of the world. They surely found what they were looking for."

Publius stood and walked to an open window, his hands meeting behind his back. Gazing out past the sheer cliffs at the villa's periphery, he said, "So that is why you are here? To ask for my intervention?"

Appius arose from his seat. "Yes, Proconsul, we ask that you send a *centuria* from your garrison to deal with these predators once and for all. We request Marcus Arcturus as the centurion, a good friend of both Rufus Flaccus and myself." Appius uttered these words directly and firmly, knowing this was likely the only chance he and his people had to save themselves.

"So many men, Appius! How could you need that many legionaries?" Publius said as he turned to face Appius, his face betraying his sadness and incredulity.

Having said almost nothing during the conversation, Lucius suddenly interrupted, his voice taut and urgent: "These are not just wolves, Proconsul Drusus. These are the malign spirits of the dead who have come upon us, driven by a vendetta against the living. My belief is that they are the *Etruscī*, returned to despoil the lands taken from them by our ancestors. But they are yet flesh and blood and can be returned to the netherworld with a sword."

Publius' heavy brow furrowed, his face now appearing almost angry instead of despondent. "Those tales of the *Etruscī* are nothing but superstition, stories to frighten unruly children," he said, the scornful annoyance in his tone evident as he waved his hand. "Wolves have preyed upon the province's herds for generations, but they are just that: wolves. Merely common beasts impelled by the need to eat and to survive." Publius turned to Appius as if for support, but was met instead by morose silence.

"I beg your pardon, Proconsul," Lucius said at last. "We have as witness one of the most trusted men in our village. He swore these wolves can walk on two legs after taking the shape of men. What he saw one night nearly sent him to Orcus." Lucius breathed in and then gulped before continuing, halfway stricken by fear as he began to retell Stephanus' story.

"Stephanus, the village cartwright and a respected elder, was on his smallholding after the attacks first began. He was outside securing his shed against the depredations of the wolves; valuables had been found missing from the village after the attacks. How mere wolves could steal coin and belongings wasn't clear, but it soon became so.

"As Stephanus barred the shed door, he spied the silhouettes of several wolves in the moonlight. They began prowling up the path to his family's villa. Stephanus stopped and hid behind the shed, not wanting to draw their attention. His wife and children had left to stay with his wife's sister in a neighboring village the day before, so the house was now unoccupied.

"Once the wolf pack reached the entrance, they began to transform, shifting and taking on new shapes. Without so much as a sound, the strange beasts assumed human form and stood upright, unclothed and unshorn. The bare, shaggy men then forced open the villa's front door, breaking the lock with only their brute strength.

"The bandits piled in and soon emerged holding a bulging sack, which was then strapped to the backs of one of the men. The house thieves fell to their knees and regained the bodies of monstrous wolves, metamorphosing in mere moments. The pack gathered and let out a blood-curdling victory howl before disappearing into the night, the clanging of Stephanus's stolen silverware ringing behind them as they fled."

Lucius paused his narrative and eyed Publius' face, but the older man gave nothing away. "Well, Stephanus was petrified in his hiding place, trembling in terror, now certain our little community had somehow brought the fury of the gods down upon us. He prayed to Lupercus that what he had seen was only a trick of a frightened mind, but in his heart he knew otherwise."

Publius studied Lucius for a moment and then moved to seat himself behind his desk. Speaking forthrightly to both men, Publius said, "I will make an offering at the temple to Apollo this evening and let the divinity speak to me through the sibyl. You will have my answer in the morning once I have pondered the sibyl's riddle. An attendant will now show you to your rooms."

Indicating an end to their meeting, Publius Drusus stood once again and turned to look out the window at the midday sun reflecting off the sparkling waters of the harbor. Appius and Lucius stepped into the hallway, finding a second attendant waiting for them. They were led across the villa's sprawling courtyard, itself lined with shrubbery and marble statuary and with a flowing fountain at its center. The attendant paused at a suite of rooms facing the courtyard and opened its door for the guests.

"So, this is where they put our satchels," Appius observed as he reached down to search their luggage. "I was worried someone had run off with them."

"What do you think?" Lucius said, an authentic bewilderment hanging over him as he sat on his mattress and watched Appius unpack. "Will Proconsul Drusus help us?"

"I believe so," Appius assured him, digging through a small leather *loculus* as he spoke. "Publius' belief in the gods is not strong, but he may listen to the oracle. My own opinion is that Publius may just be looking for a scapegoat, pinning the decision to deploy troops to the outlands on the sibyl's prattle instead of on himself."

"You don't believe in the gods, do you, Appius?" Lucius seemed almost surprised as he asked the question to his uncle.

"I believe in our family, our village, and our safety, Lucius," Appius replied matter-of-factly. "My brother and my nephew are dead, as are several other villagers. If Publius must burn some incense or 'sacrifice' nine *popona* to save us from the wolves then so be it."

"I'm going to visit the villa baths before the *cena*," Lucius said, quickly burying the subject at hand. "I'm dusty after our long journey. I just hope Proconsul Drusus didn't notice."

Lucius left the guest rooms to walk to the baths, excited to indulge in such a modern convenience. He thought back to their meeting with Publius Drusus and how the proconsul had seemed almost afraid to admit the wolves might be the vengeful spirits of the *Etruscī*.

Publius Drusus, Appius, his own father, and Marcus Arcturus had all served together in the legion, stationed at what was then the far-flung edge of the Empire.

Is there something about the wolves Appius and Publius Drusus know but are not admitting? Lucius mused as he entered the villa's *caldarium*, the heated room's hot, moist air quickly opening the pores of his dry skin. Lucius sat to remove his worn sandals and then quietly prayed, hoping his father's old friend would send aid before it was too late.

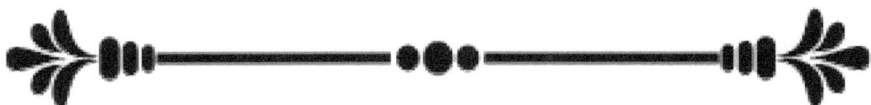

The late afternoon sun bore down on Appius and Lucius' horse-drawn cart as it entered the village's main thoroughfare, the men exhausted after their days-long journey. The villagers had been roused by the loud clacking of iron-shod wheels over the westerly hills and emerged from their simple dwellings along the wide road to watch the travelers' return.

An older man followed by a great, heavily-jowled dog opened the door to his home and approached the cart as it slowly rolled past. The dog accompanying the man bore fresh scars across its nose and cheek, evidence of the most recent wolf attack.

"*Salvē*, Appius Flaccus. Do you bring good news or bad news back with you? I pray your time with the proconsul was not wasted."

Appius drew the cart to a gradual stop, and the man reached up to put a brawny hand on his shoulder before Appius could even answer him.

"A full *centuria* will arrive in less than half a fortnight, Atticus," Appius announced, with no small measure of enthusiasm despite his weariness. "And Marcus Arcturus will lead them. The wolves will meet their end when they harass us again."

"Excellent, Appius!" Atticus said, patting Appius' shoulder in thanks. "The legion will deal with this menace. We must prepare a temporary barracks for the men before their arrival." Atticus then strode off to converse with the villagers who had gathered nearby, his guard dog in tow.

Appius urged his cart horse down to where the main road ended, finally branching off into the outlying farmsteads. His family's small villa was on the village outskirts, with its own plot of land—it had been bequeathed to Rufus

Flaccus as payment for his services to the legion. Lucius now lived with his aunt, uncle, and their children in the villa, his father and brother gone. Lucius's mother had died years before.

Lucius removed his wide-brimmed hat, hung it up, and undid the brooch holding his drab *lacerna*. His travel clothes would be stored away after laundering, he hoped for the foreseeable future. Appius was greeted by his wife, Aelia, and his children, who told him a supper had been prepared for their coming. After supper, Lucius and Appius sat outside on wood *sella* taken from the kitchen, watching a burnt orange sun set over the hills they had just traveled.

"I explored many lands in my youth as part of the legion," Appius said, breaking an uncomfortable silence after the sun had disappeared behind the hills. "But I'm sure your father must have told you some of our stories. Publius Drusus and Marcus Arcturus were valiant men, stalwarts against the *Germani* and other barbarous adversaries. Why, I remember this one time, we—"

"Father never spoke to us about his time in the legion," Lucius said suddenly, his gaze still fixed on the now-dark horizon. "He was proud of his service, but the killing... it never sat well with him. I think he was afraid he'd become used to it." Lucius looked over at Appius, unsure whether Rufus had revealed such anxieties to his younger brother.

"Rufus never flinched. He met death head-on and spit in its face. I'm sure that's how he met his end with the wolves." Appius smiled slightly as he spoke, as if recalling some act of bravery. "He must have taken a wolf or two with him."

Lucius leaned back on his stool and rested his brow in his hand. "Father did tell us one story about his coming home after a long campaign," Lucius finally said after a lengthy pause. "He probably told it to us as the story was so peculiar. You were with him if I remember correctly."

"Aye, I might recall it. Did the story involve a woman? A woman and her two sons?"

"That's the one," Lucius confirmed. "Marcus Arcturus had allowed his men to break ranks after the long campaign and leave with their own *contubernia* instead of waiting with the rest of the legion. The discharged *contubernales* passed near the borderlands of the Empire on the way home to their families.

"Even though Father was their *decanus*, you and Father broke from the other men returning home, all of them eager to see loved ones. Off from the roadside was a thatched cottage, partially hidden by the dense woods."

Appius agreed, seeming to recall more of the story now. "That's it. A strange old woman lived in that hut, half-mad, I think. But what else did your father tell you about her?"

"That she invited you in, both of you, and bid you stay the night," Lucius replied, a moment of clarity coming upon him. "She told you her own story, one about the wolves that roamed the black forestlands. She sat you next to the fire, gave you something to eat, and then began her odd tale..."

Rufus put aside his wooden spoon and began sopping up the last remnants of gruel with a thick slice of dark bread. He and Appius had eaten only early that morning and it was now close to sunset. The compatriots were tired after their long trek across the borderlands, having made most of the journey on foot. When they had spied a lonely cottage at the woodland boundary, they immediately sought shelter within.

"Gratias tibi. We appreciate your hospitality," Rufus said as he watched the woman and Appius eating, the three of them having dined in polite silence until that moment. The trio sat around a smoldering firepit, the fire's charcoal-colored smoke drifting up through a blackened hole in the straw roof of the cottage. "We're still a long way from our village," Rufus continued amicably. "This is what the imperial subjects in Aegyptus might call an 'oasis' along our journey home."

"I have little company, and you men are both in the legion. Think nothing of it," the woman replied casually, finishing with her meal and setting her bowl aside. She stood and took the men's bowls and her own to a washing basin laid on the cottage's earthen floor. Rufus observed her movements as she cleaned up, guessing her weathered appearance hid her actual age. She may even have been quite beautiful at one time, not so long ago.

"You had better check your pack mule," the woman said as she washed. "It could be a long night. The forest's edge is not safe, but I live here nonetheless."

"What's your name, woman?" Appius asked abruptly, having been quiet since taking his seat by the fire. "You've invited us in for the night, but we still don't know your name."

"I am Servilia," the woman replied, almost bothered by the question. "These lands are not my native lands, and the people who dwell past this forest are not my kin."

"I am Appius Flaccus, and this is my older brother, Rufus Flaccus," Appius said, with Rufus nodding briefly as he was introduced. "Our families are waiting for us farther along, and we hope to return to them safely. Once we have slept, we'll be on our way again in the morning."

A lone wolf howled somewhere out in the forest. Servilia looked toward the crude door of the one-room cottage and then back down at the basin, as if hoping the unsettling call would go unmentioned.

"I'll go check on our mule," said Rufus. "She could use more feed grass if we sleep past sunrise." He stood and began striding toward the cottage door, wondering why their host had ignored the sound of imminent danger not so far away.

"Wait, please. Don't venture outside just yet," Servilia pleaded, holding an outstretched hand toward Rufus. "I must tell you a story first, to help you understand why I am here, alone in these woods." Servilia gestured for Rufus to sit again by the fire, its flickering light casting shadows over her creased, weather-beaten face. "My time may soon end, and I need to pass something on to you before you take your leave of me."

Appius glanced over at his brother as Rufus took his seat on one of several decrepit wooden stools placed around the firepit. Servilia then reached under her mottled tunic to produce a silver-white coin hanging from a chain around her neck. The coin shone brightly as Servilia dangled the pendant near the light of the fire, its gleaming, argent surface in sharp contrast to the cottage's colorless, dingy interior.

"This amulet was forged in Hispania," she murmured, as if dragging forward distant memories. "It has protected me in this desolate place from what lurks at night in the forest."

Servilia then closed her hand around the pendant, suddenly breaking what was almost a hypnotic moment. Rufus and Appius were now very quiet, both feeling there was much more to this beggarly woman than they had first believed.

"I met him at the festival of the Lupercalia when I was only a girl. A man appeared in the crowd wearing the mask of the wolf. He took me and loved me. Soon after, I found I was with child—twins. The children were born in secret, away from my family, as there was no father.

"I raised my two sons alone, not far from this comfortless abode I now call my home. They grew to early manhood, and that is when the bloodlust came upon them. One day, I returned home late from the market to find two wolves, distinct from each other by the color of their coats. That this had occurred was impossible, but I knew they were my sons."

Servilia stared into the fire, lost for a moment but then flaring with sudden determination. "My sons had slaughtered our small flock of sheep in their pen. They were feeding on the carcasses when I interrupted them. One appeared ready to pounce, but the other howled into the twilight, impelling both to flee. Since that day, my sons have led the wolf packs in the hills and forests of this forsaken land."

Without pausing to mark a conclusion to the story, Servilia stood and walked to the cottage wall facing the firepit, over which hung a tattered cloth. She pulled the cloth down from its hooks to display a painting, one stained into the daub itself. It was a coarse yet vivid depiction of a she-wolf suckling two cubs, her offspring demonic and half-human in appearance.

"These demi-human beasts are cursed by the gods, avatars of revenge and depraved appetites," Servilia declared as she stood before the painting, holding forth the silver pendant. "These creatures call themselves 'the Children of Lupercus,' but they are nothing of the sort. They are infernal, and spring from the underworld itself."

Servilia stepped back toward the firepit and held the pendant before Rufus, letting it drop into his open palm. Rufus could now see the image engraved into the metal. It was much like that of the wall painting: a mother wolf with her two whelps.

"The amulet is blessed," Servilia continued vehemently, nearly shaking as she spoke, "and can seal the curse of the Luperci, trapping it in a moment of time as a moth might be cast in amber. The amulet can also act as a ward, protecting those threatened by the demons' fangs and claws."

With that, Servilia turned and let out a hacking cough, steadying herself against the wall as she did so. Facing them again, Servilia whispered, "My time is short, and they know it. The wolves close in on me. I will be too weak to use the amulet when they finally come."

Lucius turned to look at Appius in the faint moonlight, pausing the retelling of his father's story. "And then the three of you bed down to sleep, the woman's wheezing breaths soon growing shallow as she lay nearby. You and Father conspired to slip away, fearful not only that she was mad, but that she might carry the pestilence."

Stunned by the sharpness of Lucius's memory, Appius only nodded. He then said, "As we left in the dead of night, many eyes appeared outside the hut, watching us from the fringes of the forest. The wolves let us pass unmolested on the empty road, receding into the distance as we took the path home. As for what became of the woman...well. It's best not to dwell upon it."

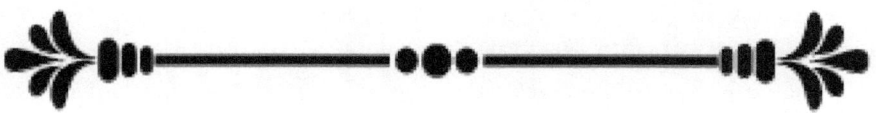

"Where did you find it?" Appius asked, studying the silver pendant that swayed gently in his grasp. He recognized the relief of the she-wolf and cubs engraved into its coin.

"In a little box, among Father's personal belongings," Lucius replied, satisfied that he'd been able to recover this lost possession. "Father was very private and kept things from his days in the legion hidden away in a chest. I would have never found it if Father were still with us." More quietly, he added, "Father may have forgotten about the amulet. It might have saved him."

"That woman was mad, Lucius," Appius scoffed. "How she came upon such a fine piece of jewelry is the only unexplainable thing from her ravings. She was destitute in that shack out in the woods."

Lucius took the pendant back from Appius. "The old woman told you this amulet was blessed. By whom, I wonder?" He looped the pendant's chain around his neck and tucked its coin under his tunic.

"The priests of Lupercus, the *Luperci*? Who knows, some divinity. I believe none of it." Appius shrugged dismissively.

"Some say that Lupercus is really Faunus," Lucius noted. "The horned god of the forest. He also relishes in playing tricks on mortals, or so it is said."

"Again, nonsense. Come, let's be about it." Appius pushed open the front door to their villa and handed Lucius a heavy *pilum,* its iron point recently sharpened. Fastening his *gladius* to his belt, Appius then led Lucius down the road to the village.

It was early evening. The howling of the wolves had kept many in the village awake the previous night, and all felt better having Marcus Arcturus and the men of his *centuria* around. They had arrived that morning and were busy preparing for the return of the wolf pack.

"*Salvē*, Marcus Arcturus. Are your men ready at their stations? The wolves attacked our people in their homes when they last came upon us." Appius embraced the imposing man in centurion's uniform as they stood at the village road's center. The man's raven hair was streaked with gray, his face marred from many long campaigns.

"We await the wolves. Forty men are sequestered in your village hall and will emerge in force once the pack begins its predations. Our war hounds are with them, collared and set." Marcus Arcturus then nodded to Lucius, acknowledging the son of his best soldier and close friend.

"Excellent. Thank you, especially for sending men to family households. Four of your men are at our villa now. Should the wolves enter, they will surely be surprised." Appius smiled broadly as he said this, hopeful that the moment of revenge was at hand.

The sun began to disappear behind the hills surrounding the village. An uneasy quiet descended, as if all knew something terrible was about to happen but none dared speak of it aloud.

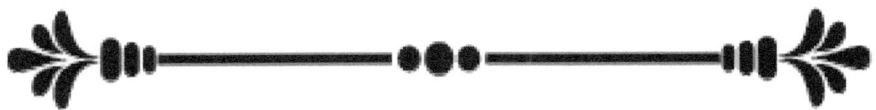

Appius and Lucius sat at the dining table with Atticus and his wife, Atticus's big dog resting at their feet.

"Your house is near the middle thoroughfare, Atticus. If the wolves come upon the road, we can rush to them and attack." Appius unconsciously put his hand over his belt as he said this, seeking the assurance his battle-worn *gladius* provided him.

A solitary wolf howl pierced the night. Distant, yes, but soon joined by a cacophony of howls much closer. Appius arose from his seat at the table just as the front door burst in violently, a sable black wolf leaping to meet his throat, the broken door falling aside.

The wolf thrashed Appius's limp body back and forth across the wooden table, blood coating the walls as Lucius reached for his *pilum*. The wolf dropped Appius from its jaws and then turned to Lucius and Atticus, finding both men armed and ready.

Baring its fangs ferociously, the wolf leaped aside as Lucius jabbed with his *pilum*. Swinging his club, Atticus was blocked by another wolf which had darted in from the village thoroughfare, the road outside now swarming with wolves of varying sizes and rustic hues.

Atticus fell under the second wolf's assault, his guard dog yowling as it was mobbed by more wolves and then brought down. Escaping through the open doorway to the road, Lucius saw what was happening: dozens, perhaps over a hundred wolves were swarming into the village, crashing against a wall of legionaries, war dogs, and armed villagers.

A soldier close to Lucius cried out as he was leaped upon by two wolves and pulled down, his *scutum* and *gladius* falling from his hands. Lucius turned and was met by an enormous auburn wolf, crouched, blood and saliva dripping from its jaws.

The wolf's great forepaws met Lucius's chest just as he reached under his tunic, knocking him back. Lucius struggled under its crushing weight, the beast's overpowering scent being almost too much to bear. With all the strength he could muster, Lucius managed to pull forth the hidden pendant with his free hand.

The pendant's coin glowed eerily with an otherworldly blue aura. The wolf recoiled and wailed, convulsing in a pantomime of excruciating pain as it fell back and then fled into the tumultuous throng around them. Recovering, Lucius pulled himself to his feet and surveyed the ongoing fray.

Bodies were strewn everywhere: some wolves, but mostly the men and dogs who had fought against them. The remaining legionaries had formed a tight circle with their *scuta* facing outward, stabbing at charging wolves attempting to break their ranks. Lucius turned and ran down the road to his family's villa, fearful his only remaining kin might also be dead.

The villa door was broken when he arrived, a bloody trail on the antechamber's floor leading away from the entrance. Lucius gripped his *pilum* with both hands and cautiously stepped into the darkened entryway. He soon found a pair of soldiers, torn and lacerated, as well as a slain wolf in the hall to the kitchen. Waves of splattered blood adorned the hallway's domestic fresco.

A low growl rumbled in the passage behind Lucius. He turned and was confronted by a sleek gray wolf a few paces away, a prominent sword gash splitting its bloodied muzzle.

The beast tensed, about to leap, just as the eerie blue light of the pendant swelled again. The wolf yelped, the sound almost pitiful, and raced away. Lucius watched it go before continuing his search. Before long, he found his aunt and the two remaining legionaries dead on the villa grounds outside.

Where are the children? Lucius thought, almost sure the wolves had taken them. His two young cousins, the daughters of Appius and Aelia, were nowhere to be seen. The villa seemed deserted now, otherwise silent save for the sounds of fighting between men and wolves, ambient in the distance. Searching further, Lucius found a torn piece of a tunic and one of the girls' loose sandals. Neither had blood on them.

The argent coin hanging from its chain glowed more brightly than ever before at this unexpected discovery, as if the pendant were attempting to lead Lucius to the girls' wolfish abductors. Lucius wandered into the night, following the faraway howling, the pendant pulling him forward.

He stumbled in the dark, the waning moon providing little illumination as he reached the low hills outside the village, trusting in pendant that shone like a floating beacon in an ocean of darkness. Soon, Lucius reached the encampment of the wolves. There, half a dozen of them lay licking their wounds around two prisoners.

The kidnapped cousins were bound and gagged, and lay resting against several sacks of stolen goods. The elder of the two girls, Norbana, saw Lucius approaching and began to struggle against her bonds, her muffled cries alerting the injured wolf pack.

Lucius strode boldly into the camp's center as the wolves arose, the pendant now blazing with a brilliant white-blue light. The wolfen creatures shrieked and howled, several limping away into the surrounding darkness, others falling and convulsing in the mud. Only one wolf, a great black beast, remained to face Lucius.

The enormous black wolf stood on its hind legs and began to reshape itself into a naked man, his ebon-hued hair matted with blood, as had been the wolf's coat. The alpha wolf, the surviving son of Servilia, reached for his blade.

"I shall kill you as a man, worthless cur," he spat, his voice harsh and venomous. "It's what one such as you deserve."

The man darted forward, slashing viciously with his curved dagger, narrowing missing Lucius's arms and throat. Lucius quickly stepped back and held the argent coin high, its unearthly bluish rays now coalescing into a loping wolf pack, translucent and ghostly in its aspect.

The celestial wolves descended from the night sky along an invisible path and thronged the man, dragging him screaming down into the earth, into the chthonian underworld of Pluto.

Lucius kept his *pilum* poised, ready for another attack, but as the moments passed in silence, he realized the daemon wolf had been cast out from this world by the noble spirits of the wolves he and his packmates had corrupted. The night on the hills was still, save for the frightened weeping of Lucius's cousins.

He reached down into the dust to pick up the pendant, having dropped it as the wolf-wraiths descended. The argent coin gleamed in the moonlight, a fresh lupine soul trapped forever within, the curse of the *Luperci* bonded with the coin's alloy.

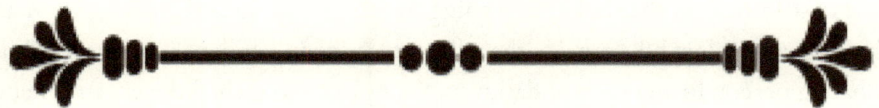

"Mere years ago, all of this was but uncultivated land for a thousand paces," Lucius enthused to the slim, smartly dressed man at his side who nodded, listening intently to his host. "My laborers and I have turned this plot into a thriving olive orchard, one which sells its produce as far away as the capital. My father never thought it was possible, but we did it." Lucius leaned on the villa balcony's balustrade, smiling at the wealthy merchant.

"I remember when your town was but a village, known mostly for its rocky soil," the man remarked blithely, his tone relaxed and casual. "You're right; what you've done here is a miracle, Lucius Flaccus, blessed by the gods." The merchant then drank from his cup, looking out from the balcony at the horizon as the summer sun dipped behind the hills. It would be nighttime soon.

"Yes, blessed by the gods. As you say." Lucius suddenly seemed absent-minded, as if recollecting a past tragedy that still haunted him. Lucius then smiled again, worried his guest might notice this fleeting moment of painful distraction.

"But it grows late, Gaius Polybius," he said swiftly, pulling himself back into the present. "My wife and one of our servants will show you to your rooms. Tomorrow we will draw up the contracts and complete the sale. *Bene quiescere.*"

The merchant nodded, bade Lucius goodnight, and stepped inside. Lucius turned back to peer out at the hills beyond. The marble balcony was one of his recent additions to his family's villa—an indulgence during this time of prosperity. Years had passed since the wolves had been driven from the village, the packs abruptly fleeing just as their victory over the legionaries appeared certain. They never returned.

The full moon was ripe and loomed large overhead as a warm breeze drifted over Lucius, helping to soothe his apprehension. Squinting into the darkness, Lucius thought he saw several shapes approaching from the road. They looked like animals, but he couldn't be sure.

Lucius kept the silver pendant in a ceramic urn high on a shelf in his bedroom, where his children couldn't reach it. His wife never inquired about the pendant, assuming it was some heirloom left to him by his father. Cursed, Lucius hoped the pendant would remain at the bottom of the urn for the rest of his days.

The wolves closed in, their sharp eyes shining in the dark, soon to reach the villa's front door.

Deep in the shaded urn, the pendant began to glow. The souls of the departed had returned, ready to take back their master's talisman.

A Hunger So...

I am the sole survivor of an unfortunate shipwreck, plunged into an unforgiving ocean during a raging storm. I was saved from certain death only by the Whim of Fate or, perhaps, an Angel of Christ's Mercy. The faithful captain of our doomed vessel - may God rest his soul - as well as our steadfast crew, only witnessed the menacing storm clouds and churning waves on the late evening horizon when it had become too late.

The storm fell upon us almost without warning, a sudden downpour followed by a punishing deluge. All were swept from the ship's deck, sending us tumbling into the eye of the tempest. That I quickly clung to some floating debris while others were pulled down into a watery grave is entirely a matter of Divine Providence and can only be explained by the Will of Our Lord.

After that dreadful night, I lay on a deserted beach, having found land as the ocean tides brought me in under cover of darkness. Amongst the briny froth, I fell into unconsciousness but then awoke to the morning sun, a reminder that I yet still lived.

The unknown island's white sands reflected brightly under my shoe-buckled feet, the cloudless sky a hue of pure azure blue. Palm trees swayed in the halcyon breeze not far from where I walked, acting as guardians to the island's lush interior. But what seemed to me like a veritable Paradise would only become a special Hell as I'll soon relate.

I stood among the pulpy detritus left along the shoreline from our former ship, *The Ascension*, picking through the shattered wood and torn sailcloth, searching for anything I could use to survive. I found a broken mast, still intact enough to be of service.

I dragged the damaged mast fixedly over the beach's sands with a plan to construct a shelter against some rocks that faced the ocean. I hadn't considered venturing into the island's tropical canopy until I was more certain of any dangers which may be present, fearing I could not be alone here on what seemed a deserted island in uncharted seas.

The mid-morning sun was quite strong, yet the air was still pleasantly mild due to the wafting breeze from the ocean. I worked feverishly, sweat beading my brow, not wanting to be caught unshielded when the sun rose even higher. But I was also thankful for the sun's brightness, for it allowed me to clearly see the task at hand.

I fashioned the mast's wood into a sturdy frame for my provisional shelter, the pieces of the mast having come apart with some effort. Gathering heavy fern leaves from the jungle's periphery, I securely thatched an improvised roof for my new home, ruefully anticipating yet another violent storm off the ocean waters.

My labor had been quick and efficient, absolute desperation driving me to toil as fast as possible. After several hours, my domicile was now complete, the rays of the equatorial sun at its zenith no longer a threat. I collapsed under the beach hut's merciful shade and surveyed my efforts; I had done well, better than I had anticipated.

I took in all that surrounded me from my resting spot: surging cerulean swells capped with white foam crashing over barren sea stacks; scattered flocks of squawking seagulls flitting through the air; the unfamiliar ocean seeming to extend out forever from these lonely, nameless shores, taunting me as the only means of escape from my archipelago prison.

This distant island was likely not found on any map. What would become of me? Was rescue something I could truly hope for, even with the Good Grace of my Savior? I had nothing other than hope now and the will to survive.

I pushed my perturbations aside as I needed both fresh water and comestible sustenance, my parched throat and empty stomach no longer tolerable. Potable water could be found only by exploring more of the island, the proximate ocean's salty brine offering nothing upon which to live, except the chance of catching some fish.

Scaling a nearby hillock, I stood and looked out over the verdant swath of the tropical forest beyond the beach's shores. The island was so large I couldn't view its entirely from my perch; the hillock may just not be of the proper elevation perhaps. More white-sand beaches framed the island's coastline to the west and to the east, but I wouldn't be able to discern the island's northern end without the aid of a spyglass, if at all.

I then caught sight of what I thought might be a pool of water amongst the dense vegetation, sunlight reflecting from it, less than a league from my observation spot. Feeling faint from dehydration, I hurried down into the jungle, trying to maintain a straight line to my goal as I strode through the snarled underbrush.

Near exhaustion and beaten down by the sun, I came to a crystalline waterfall, pouring over a cliff into its pristine basin. At last! I would have fresh water! I wasted no time.

Doffing my shoes and peeling my ragged shirt and breeches from me, I stumbled into the pool, took a few steps, and then fell face forward with a splash. My sun-burnt skin was soothed as if with a wondrous balm and I took a mouthful with both hands cupped, my long-suffering throat finally receiving a welcome reprieve.

The basin was not very deep, and I could clearly see to its sandy bottom. Wading back, I squatted in the shallows and drank as much as I could. But my stomach was still unfilled, and I worried where I might find food.

Something moved among my clothes left near the brush, seen from the corner of my eye. What was it? A small animal, black-furred. It disappeared into the jungle as soon as I leveled my gaze to where the thing had been.

Dressing, I surveyed what was around me and saw no creature. What could it have been? From what I knew of these islands' flora and fauna, few pileous beasts made their home here, most animal life being fish or feathered birds.

There must be fruits, I thought. I only need find the plants from which they hung themselves, ripe in bloom. Soon, I found a viridescent fruit growing in abundance in a forest clump not far from the waterfall, its sweet, seed-laden flesh satiating what had become a gnawing pain. The fruits sprouted from their trees' low branches and were easily harvested; I took more with me as I departed.

My ramshackle lean-to on the beach was undisturbed, just as I had left it. I planned how I would gather more food, likely searching for a different path through the jungle tomorrow. Tonight, I would have to make a fire, else I would sit only in darkness, with just the waxing moon over the nighttime waters to keep me company.

As the vivid orange sun began its low drift over the ocean, I scavenged the beach for anything of use. Chunks of wood from my ship mast had dried under the day's basking sun and were now suitable for kindling. I gathered smooth bone-white stones and laid them in a tight circle, piling wood and then clumps of grass into a heap within the stone circle's boundary.

I kept a piece of flint in a pouch under my belt, one of the few things not lost to me as I had struggled upon the ocean's surface. Some sparks from the flint stone flew onto the pile as I made use of my primitive tool, lighting a fire that then began to blaze. I sat and stared into the darting flames created from my efforts, the first manifestation of civilization I had seen since washing ashore.

I reclined in the lean-to, the crackling fire close but as not to pose a hazard, satisfied it would burn for most of the night now that the sun had set. Sleepy, I rested my head on folded hands as I lay on the sand, wishing I had a cushion for comfort.

Again, I saw it, this time through half-closed eyes. The black-furred vermin from the jungle I had witnessed earlier. As my eyes opened fully, I could now clearly see it was a smallish rat, my vision focusing in my campfire's flickering light.

The tiny creature watched me intently and, strangely, as if with purpose. It stood upright on its hind legs, its paws pendulous in front of its chest. The rat's whiskers twitched as its bright eyes reflected the nearby flames. It was sure to stay back, out of arms reach, as if it was aware I might be a danger to it.

Then, without a squeak, the rat scurried off, disappearing into the darkness of the beach at nighttime. I looked about for more of them, relieved that my visitor appeared to have been without any fellows. I worried they might come as I slept but I had some assurance the burning woodfire would keep the curious rats at bay.

I drifted into sleep, with one eye barely open, until it too finally closed in exhaustion. Dark, terrifying visions came upon me as I lay in slumber, of gnawing, ravenous maws tearing into me, devouring my weary flesh in bloody morsels. But I awoke as dawn came, whole in body, and alone on the beach, with only the morning breeze and the rising sun to greet me.

***

Surely, there must be a nest of these creatures somewhere, I thought to myself as I examined the trunk of a palm tree. Once found, I could smoke them out with a bonfire and remove this threat to my well-being, endangering my eventual rescue from the island. I needed to make a torch and then, when lit, set the rat hovel aflame, destroying the miniature devil spawn. Such was my plan.

I dried the fibers from the palm tree, torn free with care. Bundled around a stout stick from the underbrush and tied with loose fiber threads, I now had the implement I sought. When needed, I would set the torch ablaze with my flint stone, ready for its purpose.

But where were the rats and their nest? My unlit torch in hand, I returned to the waterfall, a cool respite from the growing heat of the day. As I sat by the pool's sandy bank, I surmised they could be near, as I had first seen the rat here. There had to be others, perhaps many more.

I returned to the fruit grove I had discovered earlier and searched for signs of the rats. Droppings, and nibbled, rotted gourds that had fallen to the ground from their branchlets were strewn amongst the trees. They came here to feed, likely in numbers.

After selecting a few gourds for myself, I moved some distance away and hid in the brush. I kept a watchful eye on the trees' exposed roots, rising and arching from the island's rich soil. Some time passed and as the sun waned, one appeared, and then several rats. The hungry beasts sought the partially eaten gourds in the shade where they rested and resumed their feasting.

Once its belly was full, the last rat left, and I stood to watch where the animal went as it took the grove's egress. The daylight was dim, but the rats kept to a clear path, and I espied the small black form weave between the trees and jungle greenery even as it scampered ahead with me following behind.

Not far from the fruit grove, past the foot of a high grassy knoll, stood cave rocks at considerable height. Upon these rocks a profusion of harried rats scurried up and down its cliffs, as if strained under some forced errand at the behest of an unseen Master.

Here it was! Multitudes residing therein, nests upon putrid nests! There looked to be several layers of contorted black rock but with one chasmal opening to its subterranean place, mayhap shaped by volcanic lava flows eons ago. The rats had sheltered here from the tropical sun and made this cave their home.

My original scheme was shattered. A lone torch couldn't burn the malign beasts from this underground hollow or even flush them out with billows of smoke. These caves likely extended far down, the unplumbed domain of the rats. And then there may be even more, hidden within secret recesses, skulking like cutpurses within the velvety darkness.

But at least I now knew from whence the rats came. I hoped this was their only lair on this island. How did they arrive here, so far away from Man and his Conurbations which have always sustained these parasitic things? It was a mystery I might solve by searching more of this island, most of it still unknown to me.

Making my way back to the beach dwelling, I espied a lone rat watching me, as one had done last night. The quarter-sized knave stood on its legs among the bushes, bright eyes gleaming, unafraid even though I was quite close to it. The rat's small brow furrowed unpleasantly as its snout quivered; I even imagined for a moment that the little villain sneered at me.

Turning purposefully, I left the beast behind, glancing over my shoulder only once to see the rat still watching intently. Could it know where I was going? But how could it? It was but only a simple rat, and nothing more.

I laid the gourds I had collected from the grove on a plate of palm leaves near the back of my lean-to, my torch aside. My legs folded, I sat and studied the ocean in the early evening, the tides rolling in, frothing waves crested with white foam. Was I safe? Dare I sleep tonight, even with an incessant fire shielding my slumbering form?

I realized I needed torches, and many of them. The rats en masse would eventually find me, and I wanted to burn them out before this occurred. Tossing fiery sticks into their dank nests would likely do it, ridding me of the only threat to my safety I knew of.

With the daylight I had left, I scoured the jungle environs for suitable trees, of a heavier sort than the beach palms, with the same urgency with which I had searched for food and water earlier. After some time, I came upon a ridge of verdant hills, elevated above the jungle floor. The stout trees sprouting from these hilltops were noticeably tall, their sweeping branches spread outward in all directions.

Upon reaching the first hilltop, I observed the trees here had a brownish bark covering their boles, any timber from them satisfactory as both torchwood as well as for construction of a dwelling if the need came upon me. The fallen branches I gathered were the length of my forearm, assured these castoffs would make apt incendiary pieces.

But how would these limbs burn for any length of time? A pool of pitch would provide what was necessary, but could one be found? Following the lava-fabricated mountains near to the rat caves, I came upon a gurgling black asphalt seep, situated between the hanging cliffs above.

From this heated pool, I coated the top of each branch with the blackish pitch, each wieldy stick of wood now a proper, long-burning torch in the making. The sun set as I spread the torches on flat stones not far from the beach's shore, with a mind to permit each torch's pitch overlay to fully dry and thicken. Already humid, I prayed that a rain did not come to wash away that for which I had toiled, these makeshift torches my only weapon against a marauding rat horde.

It was dark as I walked to my hut; I would need to claim the finished torches the next morning. Tonight, I would light another fire for protection as I rested. My lean-to on the beach was barely visible under the dim radiance of the moon but, as I approached, the reflecting moonlight exposed the rats, hundreds of them, swarming the place. I was unarmed, and now couldn't return home, my pitch torches not yet prepared.

I fled into the nighttime jungle, unsure of where I might hide but seeing no other recourse. The bright light of the morning sun would likely drive the rats back into their hidey-holes, but I needed to survive until then. Once ensconced in their rat den, I would recover my torches and burn the odious bastards without pity!

Running in a direction I hadn't previously sought, I made sure a good distance was between myself and the beach. I then spied and scaled a towering tree, enmeshed in the jungle's packed vegetation.

Supported by its branches, amongst hanging vines, I peered into the night, aided only by the moon overhead. From my vantage point, I saw them. Single file, racing frantically toward my hiding spot above the jungle floor, I witnessed a line of frenzied rats stretching for some distance.

Knowing the rats as able climbers and spoor trackers, I realized they would find me and be upon me without hesitation. So, crawling across the sturdy branch where I had stood, I then judged the distance to the neighboring tree, its outstretched branches nearly touching my own.

With ropey vines as support, I swung forward, tottered across a lengthy branch of the new tree, before casting myself into an open mud pit near its base. Submerged in muck, I quickly surfaced, wiping my face so my vision was unobscured. I was now bedaubed in the pungent crud, neck deep in the pit's much mire.

From down amongst the herbage, I observed a stream of black rats swarm over the branch I had just left. They milled about at the branch's end, seemingly confounded at my absence. A few dropped off, falling onto the jungle floor, but no closer to divining my whereabouts. At last, the little fiends had lost my trail!

Coated in a thick muck encasement, it clung to me as a limpet does to a tidal rock, masking my scent from the prowling rats. I pulled myself into the waiting ferns, creeping from the mud pit, the dark of night hiding my prone form. I waited until I could no longer hear the chirping of the rats and then stood to make my way into the jungle's foreboding interior.

The still sound of the jungle under a hidden moon embraced my ears, the quietness making me fearful, as if my sharp-set foe were lying in wait. Every rustle of a plant, every shadow at my outer vision, every susurrant breeze amongst the trees seemed to presage an attack by the rats, who had found me despite my efforts to elude them. I continued on this way for some time, until I saw what I thought could be the island's north shore, far from the nesting rats and their warrens.

A spreading knot of island trees waited for me, their fan-shaped fronds swaying in nocturnal winds, without companions on a high, grassy mound. Waves crashed over the beach not far from where I scaled to a place of repose, huddling myself within the bowe of the palm trees' surging stems.

Far off, I could hear the rats' tremulous twittering, as if calling to one another. Would they espy me in my safe haven? I had to risk sleep, praying my blessed Savior would guard me against these devils as I lay vulnerable. The rats' gnashing teeth setting upon my tired limbs entered my mind as I drifted out of consciousness, but the weight of slumber was too much to bear...

I blinked in the morning sunlight, relieved as I opened my eyes to a tranquil, sandy-white shore under the ocean's horizon. I had survived the night unscathed.

Now, with a clear view of the island's northernmost beach, I saw a great hull of a galleon, its masts rotten and broken, a toppled behemoth laying on its side in shallow waters. I shimmied down the palm trees' stems, landing on my feet, then walked to the beach to examine the shipwreck.

The shattered hulk was perhaps a century or more in age, I surmised, likely part of an *armada* which first explored these islands long ago. The rats must have come from this woeful wreckage, the ship's only survivors after nearly breaking apart amongst the shore's rocky outcroppings.

Still caked in a muddy shroud, I fell into the tides around the ship, washing away that which had concealed me the previous night. Sea water dripped from what remained of my tattered clothing as I strode ashore, confident my garments would dry in the hot sun.

Shielding my eyes with a hand as I stood on dry land, I scoured the lonely littoral, empty save for the enormous flotsam of the ruined ship. I spied what seemed to be the mouth of a cave, embedded in a craggy, barren cliff face. Was this a place of the rats as well? I doubted it, as the cave was so close to the sea.

I walked along the beach until I met the cave's entrance. The cave appeared shallow looking in from the outside but may have still provided shelter to someone. The vanquished galleon could have had living souls washed ashore after all.

Within, not far from its opening, were signs of occupation but not recent. The emaciated bones of a man, doubtless the only survivor who had endured from the galleon's crew, rested on a bed of withered fronds at the cave's back. The sorrowful remains bore the rags of a *conquistador's* finery, clinging to him even after many years in deathly solitude.

I found an iron axe, pitted, rusted to uselessness, hooks for fishing, and evidence wood had been hewed within the cave. Outside, under the shelter of the rocky cliffs, a braced wooden raft lay flush against the cliff walls. The raft had been purposely hidden with foliage, but now only desiccated remnants of those jungle plants covered its bare planks.

If, perhaps, sinewy vines replaced the decaying rope lashed between the raft's logs for reinforcement, the raft might still be usable. Here it was, my means of escape from this accursed island of shipwrecks! I need only gather those vines, bind them to the raft, and then drag the seaworthy vessel into the waters off these shores. I could be cresting the ocean waves by the next sunrise!

I labored during the sweltering day in the jungle close to the beach, knowing hunger and thirst, but carried aloft by the prospect of my looming freedom. I now had enough strong, fibrous vines to fortify the raft, ensuring her log beams would remain together during my trip over deep waters.

Working quickly, I tied the vines to the raft's logs, fastening them taut. I would only know if the raft was truly seaworthy once pushed out into the ocean but that would need wait. The rats! Their numbers must be culled before I leave this island.

These creatures are clearly abominations, gifted with some strange intelligence, perhaps even diabolical in nature. I should put them to the flame, leaving none alive if it be within my power to do so. All I have seen is the Hand of Lucifer at work. Cleansing this place of this evil was my blest duty as a Follower of Christ.

I found the pool of refreshing water near the grove of the gourd fruits after travelling back from the north of the island. I drank for some time and then rested on the wet sand, hoping the remaining daylight was enough for my task. I gathered gourds from the grove and ate several of them, knowing I would be able to carry scarcely any food with me when I returned to my raft.

The pitch torches I had prepared were undisturbed, lying in a row on the flat rocks where I had left them. Palm fronds and loose branches were a burden, but I collected as many as I could, holding all of it in my outstretched arms as I advanced toward the lava caves of the rats.

These terrible vermin feared the pure sun and, on this day, the tranquil blue sky over the island was empty of clouds. Cloistered in their sunless cavern, I intended to roast the rats alive in their foul lair but first I must plumb its depths. With a heap of kindling near to the cave's mouth, I entered, a solitary torch lighting my way as I trod along dark paths.

The light from the sun outside was soon swallowed up by the darkness of the cave, my torch blazing, casting outlandish shadows about its walls as I took deliberate steps. I caught the faint echoes of scuttling and the chirping of rats, the contours of a darting form sometimes appearing large against the earthen passageway into which I trod.

As I moved farther into the caves, the stone walls glistened, as if coated with a sickening, oily lubricant. I held my torch to the wall closest and noted a thin black ooze of sorts covered much of its surface, rippling ever so slightly as if in response to the heat of the torchlight.

These caves could go very deep indeed, even into the bowels of the World herself, this island being only the fertile top of an expansive mountain reaching out of the waves and into the vast ocean. Whatever is here could be quite ancient, from a time before Man ever sailed the seas or even strode upon the good soil of Our Lord's Creation.

The long passage seemed to come to an end, another arched opening in the stone of the cave not far ahead of me. I stepped through and found a narrow ledge, the precarious cusp of a spiraling pit. Beneath my feet, I looked down, my torch illuminating a sight of unspeakable horror.

A seething, undulating mass of black fur and open jaws filled the pit below, the many hundreds of rats clawing over each other, ensnarled in a twisted web of rattish carnality. From the cave ceiling above, something fell and landed on the ledge close by to me, momentarily pulling my eyes from the horror in the pit.

I held my torch over what had fallen, my vision limited in this abyssal recess. It was a black glob near to the size of my hand, its substance alike to what I had seen on the passage walls leading to this place. Again, as with the slimes along the walls of the passageway, the glob appeared to recoil under my burning torch, its lacquered skin perturbed by the torch's wounding flames.

My head tilted upward, and I saw from whence the strange blob had come: the stone ceiling above the rat pit was overspread with the black goo, its moist folds surging, the otherworldly putrescent grot ebbing and flowing around lava-formed stalactites, born of a molten inferno.

The hand-sized glob at my foot then crept away, crawling up the walls of the cave to meld with the cowl of cascading ooze hanging over me. The black slime was alive, feeding on or even guiding the rats below it. The rats had bred here in the unseen entrails of the cave's deepest part, shaped and nurtured by an alien intellect dredged from within the Earth's antediluvian crust.

I ran from the disgusting pit, the withering flames from my dying torch leading me back to sunlight and my bunches of kindling. I took to the task of piling the wood and fronds into the passage leading back to that place, praying the fire and smoke would kill the Hell's spawn rats and the Hadean monstrosity which festered above them.

The chirping of the rats had grown into a great turmoil as I piled the last of the tinder onto the heap; perhaps the subterrene entity had warned them of my intent, this aberration sensing the thoughts and animus of those around it. Torch after pitch torch, I tossed them one after the other into the now burning accumulation.

Panic-stricken rats had begun to emerge into the passageway when I flung the final torch into the freshly blazing bonfire. Without hesitation, I charged toward the cave's entrance, charred vapors from the rats' funeral pyre smothering the tunnelways I had left behind me.

There, in the bright light of the sun, I watched as pillars of choking black smoke issued forth from the cave's stony orifice, the horrible shrieking of the rats manifest even from the cliffs where I stood. The fiends were done, painfully suffocated in their loathsome abysmal demesne.

I would make my journey over the ocean this night, not wishing to linger much longer. That I would be able to subsist on rainwater and the raw fish of the sea was my hope. I prospected a miserable death by starvation or thirst, but I could no longer remain on this friendless island, castaway from those I loved and from all which my heart holds most dear.

My raft rested above the rolling waves near the shore, bobbing steadily on the limpid ocean waters of the shoal. The gourds I had would nourish me for a few days and I had taken the fishing hooks from the cave of the *conquistador*, with but sparse jungle vines to thread them.

The sun was starting to set. I resolved to forage the *conquistador's* cave a final time, yearning for the chance of procuring something to aid my trip. Not much light was left for this day, but the cave was small, and I knew it well now.

I searched through the back of the cave, my eyes squinting in the dismal light. Under a reddish stone was a depthless crevice, not much deeper than the length of my hand. In it rested a bundle of brass twine, attendant cords for the *conquistador's* fishing hooks! Hidden well, the man must have made use of the twine only when truly needed, until his time had past.

I heard a squeak from somewhere behind me. Soon more sharp, high-pitched squeaks followed, the shapes of many rats gathered in the shadows of the cave's threshold.

Running, I leapt over the teeming rats who had gathered to block my way but hundreds more were outside. How had they escaped? At least some should have perished in the caves but there must have been legions more of these black furry devils, emplaced elsewhere.

Rats clambered up all sides of my exposed leg, hissing as they bit and scratched. The pain from the small bites and claws was dull but I knew I was in grave danger. The thronging rats would devour me, without a morsel left, if they managed to bring me to ground.

Violently shaking them loose, the rats scattered as I lunged across the beach and dove into the waters close to my raft. I pulled myself aboard, clutching the brass twine from the cave. Having contrived an oar from a heavy tree branch, I paddled mightily, guiding the raft over the tumbling waves and out to sea.

The rats gave dogged pursuit, swimming into the ocean and scrambling onto the raft's stern. I swung in an arch, swatting them with my oar, sending some flying back into the water while others were crushed into bloody heaps. Along the beach, I espied a large form, striding head and haunches above the innumerable rats who still milled about onshore.

The thing I saw was a monstrous black rat, with the immensity of that of a Wolfhound, the apparent King of the assembled mass. The Rat King's eyes overflowed with the same black ooze I had seen on the walls of the rat pit, as if the thinking Filth had taken this rat as its vessel and then had grown it to a preternatural size.

The Rat King, its eyes black-within-black, then stood upon its hind legs as it saw me. Dominant over its teeming minions, the aberrant Beast let out an unspeakable roar as I sailed into the red sun of day's end, buoyed by the rising tide out to sea. I had denied the Beast its prey, perchance avoiding the fate of Possession, taken into the viscous folds of a Horror from the very depths of the Netherworld itself.

The dying sun finally slept, and I lay upon my raft, the ocean waves beneath me chopping over its sides. As I drifted over dark waters, I prayed to Our Lord and Savior that I would soon be found, and that these strange rats and their subterranean Master remain on their forsaken island, where Man may never again encounter them.

Forged in Fire

Preston Winscott folded his copy of *The Times*, having just read the front-page news. There had been another murder at the city docks, this one as gruesome as the last. For months, a vicious killer had terrorized the city, slaying apparently at random. The victims all occupied lower social strata but otherwise had nothing in common. All had been found with missing organs and all had died with their throats ripped out. The police had no suspects and no leads, so the killer remained at large.

"You, young Winscott, have you read about the latest homicide down by the docks?" Gerald Hoskins approached Winscott as he sat in their club's drawing room on one of its palatial leather seats. Winscott had recently been inducted into the gentlemen's society of which they were both members. "This time, it was a street hawker," Hoskins continued, in his characteristic gruff manner. "The poor boy was found lying among his newspapers and wares. A bloody mess, like the others."

"Yes, Mr. Hoskins, I'm afraid I have," Winscott replied as he looked up at the older man. "This is the fourth victim now, isn't it?" Hoskins was a club officer and a close confidant of its founder, John Fallada. "*The Times* has been following the case. It's all been very sensational."

"I hope they catch him soon. Whomever it is is a madman and deserves to hang," Hoskins said pointedly. He then walked away, seating himself among several other society members engaged in riotous conversation, their copies of *The Times* in hand or nearby.

Winscott had joined the Argentum Club to socialize with others who shared his interest in natural science and the arts. A newly graduated medical doctor, Winscott was a man of relatively modest means but had nonetheless been inducted by the members with unanimous support. Owing to his quick mind and encyclopedic knowledge of the biological sciences, Winscott had won entry into the society where many others of his age and social standing had been turned away.

Taking out his pocket watch, Winscott checked the time: he needed to be back at the surgery in one hour. Winscott left the club and walked several blocks to a horse-drawn tram. He rode it back to the city hospital where he was employed. His mentor at the hospital, Doctor Arthur Burton, was waiting there for him.

"Doctor Winscott, so good of you to join us. You're late." Doctor Burton stood with the trainees in the surgery, their patient under anesthesia lying between them on the table. "You'll only need observe; this is a procedure you haven't yet needed to attempt outside of your studies."

The room reeked of bodily fluids. *The man on the table must have an infected limb*, Winscott decided. The patient was aged and bare under the white cloth that covered his midsection. Winscott placed a handkerchief over his nose and watched as a trainee doctor opened a leg wound, yellowish-white pus oozing forth from it. A second trainee doctor gagged, his mouth covered by a hanky.

After their session, Doctor Burton asked Winscott to meet him in his offices adjoining the surgical room. "Next time, you'll have to perform the same procedure by yourself while under my observation," Doctor Burton told him.

"The medical profession has made great progress these last few decades, I'm happy to say," Doctor Burton enthused. "That man would have likely lost his limb under unspeakable agony if we hadn't been able to sedate him and treat the inflammation." Doctor Burton slipped a vest and suit coat over his clean linen shirt before sitting.

"Medical school opened my eyes to these advances, Doctor Burton. I can only imagine what this new century may bring," Winscott said warmly, having already seated himself before Doctor Burton's desk.

Doctor Burton seemed concerned, as if his mind carried a heavy weight. "Winscott, you're aware of these terrible murders taking place around the city docks, are you not? The victims have all been found mutilated." Doctor Burton paused, peering into Winscott's face as if waiting for his reply.

"Why, yes, of course, Doctor Burton. The entire city is on edge over the homicides. I've been reading *The Times* for daily updates." Winscott thought it odd that Doctor Burton would even ask; everyone had heard of these murders. They were without precedent in the city's recent history.

"You're right. I only wanted to put into context what I'm about to tell you," Doctor Burton said, a hint of trepidation entering his voice. "I've been in contact with the commissioner at Scotland Yard and the detectives assigned to the case. Certain details have been made available to the newspapers, while others haven't. As head surgeon here, I've helped perform the autopsies on the deceased victims in each instance." Doctor Burton was now noticeably uncomfortable—a slight sheen of sweat glimmered on his forehead, and he kneaded his fingers into his palms.

Winscott frowned, afraid of where the conversation was going. "The articles have mentioned organs extracted from those killed, which is bizarre in and of itself," Winscott remarked, "but what else could have been left out if the police were willing to divulge such a morbid particular?"

"The police could only hide so much about the conditions of the bodies as the victims' remains were found by members of the public. However, the autopsies I completed on the dead have revealed a horrifying detail: the missing organs were likely eaten—directly from the wounds of the deceased." Doctor Burton's previously worried expression became one of visceral disgust.

"Why, that's horrible," Winscott blurted out. "So, the police are dealing with not only a killer but a cannibal as well?"

"Yes, it appears so. The detectives considered consulting an alienist, but for now they want to know if we have ever found any bodies that had been defiled like this. The remains dredged up from around the docks area often end up here," Doctor Burton explained, relieved to finally tell another the terrible secret he had been holding close to his chest.

"So, if I may ask, why are you telling me this, Doctor Burton? I would surmise that this is information the police would want to keep hidden from the public. As head of surgery, you should be able to let the police know what they need to help solve the murders." Winscott didn't want to seem insubordinate, but he was surprised Doctor Burton would relate any of this to him at all.

"Winscott, the police have reason to believe the murderer is possibly connected to the society you've recently joined, the Argentum Club," Doctor Burton revealed. "The only witness has been kept out of the papers in the hopes the killer will become overconfident and careless. The witness claims to have seen a man leave the docks near the scene of a killing before returning to your club. It was the most recent murder, from last week."

"Who is the witness that the police are protecting?" Winscott queried, now intrigued by all of this, even though his previous fear was not yet relinquished.

"No name was provided to me, of course, but the witness is another street hawker, a companion of the young boy who was slain," Doctor Burton confided. "He followed a man he described as 'dressed as a fine gentleman'—that is, wearing a top hat and cape. The man headed through the night streets to the back of the Argentum Club. The man slipped through a door behind the club, apparently.

"On this particular night, a heavy fog had set in, preventing the boy from seeing more than how the man was dressed," Doctor Burton continued. "The boy later reported his dead friend to the police. He had heard screaming, but by the time he arrived, there was only the suspicious gentleman leaving an alley nearby. As you can imagine, a gentleman would be quite out of place in that down-market part of town."

"So, what do the police want me to do? You've just described nearly every member of the club: 'a top hat and cape.' There must be a few hundred members now. The club has grown so much over the last twenty years." Winscott seemed rather proud as he relayed this fact.

"And I'm sure much of that is due to the prominence of your club's founder, Mr. Fallada," Doctor Burton said plainly. "That's the other issue: the police only have the word of a young boy, and an impoverished one at that. They can't search the club and question its members based on the unsubstantiated accusation of an urchin.

"Besides, Mr. Fallada is quite wealthy—he could possibly buy immunity for one of his members unless a compelling case is leveled against him. It's all just too much for the police to manage themselves, and this is their only lead, however tenuous. If you have any suspicions or observe anything, they want to know about it." Doctor Burton then gave Winscott a hint of a smile, hoping to gain his assent.

"Well, I'll do what I can. I'm still a junior member and I'm not privy to all that much. If I see or hear anything dodgy, I'll tell you right away." Winscott hoped Doctor Burton would be pleased with this answer and then just forget about the entire matter. The idea that one of the Argentum Club members, all accomplished men in their respective fields, was stalking the city docks, slaughtering the downtrodden, and then cannibalizing their remains seemed preposterous.

"By the way: *Fallada*. What kind of name is that? He's certainly not a member of the gentry. Is Mr. Fallada a foreigner?" Doctor Burton was polite when he said this but seemed more than simply curious.

"He has foreign roots, I'm told, but was born here," Winscott replied, casually repeating what he had heard from club members. "It seems he's descended from an Iberian princeling or something of the sort. His family made their fortune in precious metals generations back."

After attending to patients and completing his rounds, Winscott left the hospital later that evening. The fog was thick in the city streets, rolling past him as he walked to his residence nearby. *If the killer is a member of the Argentum Club, who might it be?* pondered Winscott, brushing the idea from his mind almost as soon as he thought of it.

The crowd was larger than Winscott had supposed it would be. Perhaps fifty or more people were facing the low stage: nearly a packed house. Winscott was skeptical about being here at all, let alone about the likelihood of learning anything worthwhile. His fellow member of the Argentum Club, Foster, had invited him to this demonstration on mesmerism. Winscott regretted attending as soon as he sat down near the stage, his chair in the front row.

"There you are, Winscott." Foster stood in the room's threshold, dressed in his winter suit. "I'm so glad you could make it. I'm sure you won't be disappointed." All smiles, Foster took the empty seat next to Winscott and then scanned the room behind them. "Quite a turnout. The mesmerist should be here soon."

"Why did I let you invite me here, Foster? And why do you believe in this fashionable nonsense," Winscott lamented, asking the second question in a lower tone of voice. "Aren't you a naturalist? You should be pressing butterflies, not obsessing over this bunk."

A woman sitting behind Winscott whispered sharply to her male companion as if angered by the opinion Winscott had just expressed.

"Just have an open mind, Winscott. Once you witness a demonstration of mesmerism, you'll be completely convinced of its veracity." Foster then stood to greet someone sitting nearby. Several minutes passed before he returned, nearly levitating with anticipation.

Soon, a man arrived on stage, smartly dressed and carrying a compact leather briefcase. He placed the briefcase on the table at the stage's center. On either side of the table stood a plush velvet chair, much like those used by the audience.

The man opened the briefcase and took out several items he then placed on the table, too small to be seen clearly from where Winscott was seated. The man then turned to the assembly and raised his arms in welcome.

"Good evening, ladies and gentlemen. I'm so glad that you have come. My name is Alexander Beaumont. I was both a protégé and close confidant of the late Madame Obolensky, as well as a senior member of her Society of Harmony. Her society for the inquiry into spiritual matters and life after death continues after her recent and most unfortunate demise.

"This evening, I will provide a demonstration of the enlightened science of mesmerism, of which both Madame Obolensky and I are—were, in her case—ardent devotees. The practical application of mesmerism can cure physical ailments, heal the broken mind, and reveal secrets of which even the subject may be unaware.

"All I ask for is a volunteer from the audience, chosen at random, who is willing to show everyone gathered here today the power of this technique and demonstrate what it can do for the healthy and afflicted alike."

A young woman in the audience stood up immediately, calling out, "Me, Mr. Beaumont. I volunteer." She then strode confidently toward the stage and stood next to Beaumont, waiting for permission to take the seat next to the table.

Beaumont seemed surprised, as if he hadn't anticipated such an eager response. "All right then, Miss. What's your name, if I may ask?"

The young lady replied enthusiastically, "Penelope Matthews, at your service."

The audience chortled in response, enamored at this fetching young girl's bravado.

"Pleased to make your acquittance, Miss Matthews. Now, please, remove your fine hat—place it on the table here—and sit very still in this chair." Beaumont then reached for one of the objects he had left on the table earlier.

Penelope seated herself and Beaumont took the other chair, facing her. He produced a coin pendant on a silver chain which dangled as he held it. "Relax and breathe out slowly, Miss Matthews. I'm going to mesmerize you with this charm. You will go to sleep, and when you wake, you will remember none of this. But when I tell you to wake up, you'll awaken instantly."

Staring fixedly at the oscillating pendant, Penelope became quickly and visibly heavy-lidded as the charm swayed rhythmically in Beaumont's grasp. She slowly entered a state of repose, and the audience hushed as they watched, spellbound.

Winscott whispered softly to Foster, "What's that necklace he's using? It looks ancient."

"I don't know," Foster murmured. "The coin on the chain might be from a museum."

"Now, Miss Matthews, you are asleep," said Beaumont in a calm, steady voice. "Please, tell me, are you asleep, Miss Matthews?"

Penelope answered Beaumont in a faraway voice, "Yes, I am asleep."

A low gasp rippled through the audience as they heard her reply.

"Good. Miss Matthews, we're going to go back into your past: to any place or time before this one. Allow your mind to wander and find a memory. Once you've found it, please tell me what it is and where you are." Beaumont still held the silvery pendant, but it was now hanging loosely from his hand.

Penelope's head began to turn back and forth as it rested against the back of the chair. Her lips began to move until, steadily, sounds emerged. "I'm somewhere in a dark forest. I'm chasing something, running very fast."

Beaumont remained calm. "Miss Matthews, please tell us more. Is there anyone with you? What are you chasing in those woods?"

"I'm not myself... I'm something else," Penelope replied, her voice sharpening, growing loud and shrill. "There are wolves around me. Large black wolves. It's night, and we're hunting."

There were audible gasps from the audience. Winscott looked around; many seemed visibly startled or upset.

Beaumont was taken aback, as if this was entirely unexpected. "Miss Matthews, are you sure that this is your memory and not just a bad dream? How do you know that this is you?"

Penelope's head turned back and forth as before. Abruptly, she stopped. Her eyes shot open. Her pupils were gone, her irises now completely white, as if she were blind. Penelope then growled in an animalistic voice, "Let me show you."

Leaping forward from her chair, Penelope grabbed Beaumont by his throat, sending them both tumbling to the stage floor in a clatter. Snarling savagely, Penelope clawed at Beaumont's eyes and bit at his face, the stunned Beaumont defenseless as he lay sprawled on his back.

Men from the audience rushed to Beaumont's aid while others ran screaming from the conference room. One woman fell to the floor in a faint. Three men had to pull Penelope from Beaumont, his face bloodied as she flailed wildly.

Beaumont climbed to his feet and cried, "Penelope, you will wake now!" Penelope abruptly went limp in the arms of the men who had restrained her. She slowly opened her eyes and, seeing the blood covering Beaumont's face, recoiled in disbelief.

Wiping his face with a cloth handkerchief, Beaumont winced and then asked the men to let go of Penelope.

"Are you sure, sir? This madwoman nearly killed you." The bearded man in a black suit held Penelope cautiously, a hand under one of her arms.

"Miss Matthews isn't at fault. The mesmerism session must've gone awry. Please, place her in the chair and let her go. She is her sweet young self again." Beaumont examined his face with his fingers, touching shallow slash wounds and wincing in pain once more.

The men carefully put Penelope back in her chair by the table and stood guard nearby. Penelope looked about the room before burying her face in her hands, sobbing uncontrollably.

Winscott and Foster had watched all of this unfold, too surprised to have intervened in time. Winscott saw the silver coin pendant lying on the floor near the stage, cast aside during the utter chaos that had unfolded mere moments before. The image on the silver coin was that of a she-wolf suckling her two cubs. Before anyone could see him, Winscott snatched up the pendant and quickly left the room.

"That was quite a ruckus at the Arts Club. One of their open conferences for discerning members of the public, I presume." Doctor Burton spoke to Winscott from behind his desk, having recently returned from the surgery. His mood seemed to have improved since their last encounter, when he had first told Winscott about the cannibal killer.

"That poor woman who went mad is in an asylum now, at least temporarily. And we both know what it's like in there." Winscott thought back to that evening, disquieted at the shocking scene he had witnessed.

"Well, Winscott, do you have anything for the police? I mean, do you have any suspects at the Argentum Club so far? Even anything uncertain you've seen?" Doctor Burton seemed hopeful.

"No, nothing," Winscott replied offhandedly. "I think the police may have been led astray by that street urchin. There hasn't been another murder by the docks since last month and I've found no reason to suspect anyone at the club." Winscott believed this answer would satisfy Doctor Burton, finally.

"You know, the police detective working on the case brought something quite interesting to my attention," Doctor Burton said carefully, his eyebrows rising as he spoke. "Every time there's been a murder by the docks, it's been on a night when the moon was full. The victims were found early that morning or during the day, but it seems the murders were done under the moon's full illumination. The newspapers haven't yet picked up on this pattern."

Winscott appeared puzzled. "When's the next full moon?"

Doctor Burton replied, "On Christmas Day. Will there be a gathering at your social club then?"

"Yes, but likely early in the evening," Winscott answered. "Married members will be at home with their families soon afterward. Since I'm still a bachelor, I'll probably remain longer. There will likely be a few revelers staying late, with nowhere else to go."

"Stay and see if you notice anyone leaving late," Doctor Burton requested, then becoming quiet for a moment as if unsure whether to ask some troubling question. Finally, he said, "Can you tell me more about Fallada?"

"Why do you ask? Do you suspect him?" Winscott again seemed puzzled.

"No, I don't suspect anyone," Doctor Burton reassured Winscott. "It's just that there's more to his background than most realize, including your club members. There are reasons to believe he's a naturalized citizen, not native-born, and that his family has rather unsavory connections—more than most might suspect. I have contacts in the Civil Service, and they did the necessary research for me."

"I've only met Mr. Fallada once," Winscott stated distantly, remembering the past encounter. "When I was first inducted into the society. He was a very well-spoken, charming man, quite supportive of my candidacy. But he's not really there all that much, it seems. Generally, it's Mr. Hoskins who keeps things running."

"Well, keep an eye on Mr. Hoskins as well," Doctor Burton urged. "We'll see if anything comes of Mr. Fallada soon. The police are going to stake out the docks on Christmas Day and station an officer outside of the Argentum Club. But the docks are such a large space, and they only have so many men.

"If you see Mr. Fallada or anyone else leave the club alone late that night, please follow him and see where he goes," Doctor Burton further enjoined, his voice becoming low. "The police can't spare any more men on what is only guesswork at the moment. They'll be working undercover, not in uniform."

Walking up the steps to the Argentum Club's front doors, Winscott noted the busy street beyond. Tonight, there would be a Christmas social, and Winscott would see John Fallada and many other members of the club in one place.

A magnificent Christmas tree stood in the drawing room's center, the room's rich furniture having been moved aside to make space for it. Winscott observed club members beginning to congregate. Many were served drinks from trays by demure waiters, and all spoke haltingly among themselves. Winscott reached into his suit breast pocket and touched the silver pendant, still unsure whether it was to blame for that young woman's transformation into a rabid beast.

Winscott continued surveying the drawing-room, pondering who the killer might be, assuming he was here at all. Most club members were entirely unassuming, so it did little good speculating on their criminal natures without evidence. These men possessed no peculiarities that might implicate them in the murders. As for those who did stand out, they hardly seemed the murderous sort. There were several, however, who did warrant consideration—and they were at the Christmas party tonight.

There was Mr. Stevenson, who had a very unpleasant personality and had often made unfavorable comments about "the lower classes." But violent enough to have committed these murders? Almost unbelievable.

Then there was Mr. Chapman, who was quite a suspicious character, making queer pronouncements and slinking about at gatherings. But he was more of an eccentric and not someone who could be considered dangerous. Just an oddball.

And then there was Mr. Hoskins. Short-tempered, coarse to the point of rudeness at times, and always keeping irregular hours. The last one to leave the club at night, almost without fail, but usually to his waiting carriage. It wasn't unimaginable that he could take a life but, again, the carnage around the docks was beyond what even a man like Mr. Hoskins was capable of. *There's probably no killer here at all*, decided Winscott.

Winscott then saw Mr. Fallada enter the room—it was only the second time he had seen him in person. Silver-haired and wearing a charcoal-gray suit, Fallada beamed as he strode in, greeting club members earnestly and then joining Mr. Hoskins near the bar cart. He leaned in to speak into Mr. Hoskin's ear for a moment, then left to converse with someone else.

As the early evening hours passed, club members began to leave for their homes and private family celebrations. Mr. Fallada approached Winscott to welcome him. "Winscott, it's so good of you to make an appearance at our annual Christmas soirée. The new members often consider this event optional. I can assure you that it is not."

"I'm pleased to be here, Mr. Fallada. I wouldn't have missed the club's Christmas social for anything." Winscott tried to smile as Fallada shook his hand, but the older man's intensely steady gaze made Winscott uncomfortable. Shooting a quick glance away from Winscott's face and down toward his chest, Fallada then walked away without saying another word.

Foster had been watching the pair. He walked up from behind Winscott and said, "So, how are you, old boy?" and slapped him on the back. "I haven't seen you since the debacle at the Arts Club. I hope you don't blame me for what happened."

"No, not at all. No one could have seen that coming. I'm still just a bit worried about the girl, that's all." Winscott wanted to give Foster his attention, but he was still distracted by his unsettling exchange with Fallada only moments ago.

"Her parents should be able to extricate her from the asylum soon. As I understand it, the alienists want to ensure she's not a threat before releasing her." Foster gave a tight smile. "So! Any plans for later this evening?"

"I think I'm going to stay late here. Enjoy the holiday festivities and all that." Winscott was able to smile this time—he hoped that would be enough to make Foster leave him alone.

"There won't be too many left later tonight. Only old Hoskins and the other hangers-on. See you around the club again soon, what?" Foster turned his back and then made his way toward the open doors leading to the foyer.

The hours passed, and club members continued to leave, with Winscott finally standing near the Christmas tree by himself. Mummers could be heard out in the street going from door to door, bringing seasonal cheer:

We wish you a merry Christmas,

And a happy New Year,

A pantry full of good roast beef,

And barrels full of beer.

As the mummers' caroling faded away, Winscott noticed Hoskins pass through a curtain that led up a small flight of stairs to the club officers' personal chambers. Rank-and-file society members were only allowed on the club's second floor for induction ceremonies and other official matters.

What could Hoskins be doing? Winscott wondered as he watched his acquaintance pull the crimson red curtain aside, briefly revealing the steps leading up, and then vanish. *I've only ever seen him leave the club through the front doors and then take his carriage. And nothing's going on upstairs this late, that's for sure.*

Thinking quickly, Winscott decided to take a chance. He looked around and, confident the coast was clear, casually strolled toward the red curtain. With a final glance over his shoulder, he parted it and slipped inside. The sound of Hoskins' footsteps echoed from the floor above, and Winscott heard a door close.

The upstairs club room was empty, with the doors to the small private chambers along its hallway shut. *The door sounded like it was closed back here*, Winscott considered. He walked down a cramped staircase leading to a narrow back door. It was locked, and Winscott slid the bar loose before quietly cracking the door open and slipping his head out.

Soup-like fog rolled over the cobblestone street connected to the alleyway. The light from the full-risen moon remained mostly obscured by clouds drifting overhead, but nonetheless Winscott spied the silhouette of Hoskins walking slowly into the night, alone. Stepping into the alley, Winscott shut the door behind him and began following Hoskins at a distance.

Winscott skirted the glow of gaslight streetlamps, keeping to the shadows. Eventually, Hoskins entered an alley close to the docks district. Winscott stopped across the street, sheltered by an unlit shop's threshold. He hoped Hoskins would come out soon.

Instead, a guttural growl pierced the night, followed by a hideous cry and, finally, the sound of flesh being rended. Winscott remained tightly hidden as the screaming continued, panicked that he had found the real killer.

The screaming stopped and from the alley emerged a man dressed in a top hat and cape. He paused for a moment, looking both ways down the empty street. The man then slipped out of view, disappearing into the thick fog which billowed around him.

Hesitating, Winscott wondered if he should check the alley Hoskins had entered, almost sure of what he would find. *A dead end*, he thought, gulping, *no other way out*. He cautiously walked across the now silent street and peered into the gloomy alleyway, seeing what looked like mangled human remains among the dustbins and debris.

Hoskins, why him? Why was he out here all by himself? Winscott gasped as he began to retrace his steps, lost otherwise, following street signs and city landmarks back to the Argentum Club. He found the backdoor unlocked and stepped inside, standing in the dark space at the bottom of the stairs.

A light shone from the floor above. The stairway creaked as Winscott ascended, feeling both curious and afraid. It was past midnight; who could be at the club this late?

One of the chamber doors was cracked open, the room's light pouring out into the hallway. Winscott quietly moved toward the door, pausing a few paces from the entrance.

He heard a voice, Fallada's: "Please come in, young Winscott. I know that you're there."

Winscott froze in place, his legs made of stone.

"Don't just stand there in the hallway. Please do come in."

The door creaked open wider, as if moved by unseen hands. Winscott peeked inside and saw Fallada slipping on his suit coat, grinning. "Yes, come in. I've been waiting for you."

Winscott stepped inside. Fallada stood in front of him at his desk, wearing the same gray suit as earlier in the evening.

"I know you have the amulet. Please give it to me," Fallada requested, still grinning, the upright palm of his hand now outstretched.

"What happened to Hoskins? Was that you in the alley tonight?" Winscott sputtered in response, overwhelmed by what was happening to him.

"Hoskins had to be removed, I'm afraid. He knew too much about what happened with Madame Obolensky. Even after her death, she still has many devoted followers, and they were beginning to grow suspicious." Fallada let his hand fall to his side.

"Madame Obolensky? Were you responsible for her death?" Fear was starting to overcome Winscott, but he remained steadfast. He thought his life might depend on it.

"Yes. But 'Madame Obolensky' was actually a pseudonym. Her accent, as well as her entire persona, were affected. The woman was a charlatan and a quite well-paid one. But she *did* have this in her possession before I took it from her." Fallada reached into his breast pocket and produced a silver pendant, identical to the one recovered by Winscott at the mesmerism session.

"The old fraud had no idea what she really had at her bosom. But I did. Using this sacred artifact to perform mere parlor tricks . . ." Fallada shook his head, his face showing obvious disgust.

"You're the killer, Fallada," Winscott said firmly, angered that he could have been led into this web of deceit. "The police—they will corner you and eventually bring you to justice. But your charm, what does it do for its owner? Why would you kill to get it from that mystic?"

"This charm, as you call it, was forged in fire by my ancestors many generations ago. Indestructible, except in the place where it was created. The pendant was then lost for centuries, but we made every effort to find it. When we recently learned the silver pendant was held by Madame Obolensky, I took the necessary action," Fallada said, his expression gloating.

"But what does it give its user, you ask? Power. And immortality. To be free, and to be powerful, and, of course, to live forever. I am and will be forever, a true apex predator," Fallada declared, his eyes wide with exhilaration. "Now, if you please, Winscott, your silver pendant. As I said, I know you have it." Fallada grinned and stretched out his hand once more.

"How can we both have the pendant?" Winscott asked, panting, backing away as he touched his suit breast pocket. "Or is mine a copy?"

"A forgery, yes. Created by Madame Obolensky's disciples. But apparently with properties of the original, as the Arts Club found out. Now, please . . ." Fallada took a step forward, no longer grinning.

Winscott turned as if to run, but Fallada's words held him rooted to the spot. "Oh, don't try to leave, young Winscott. The outside doors are all locked. I've seen to that. You won't be getting out of here—not alive, at least."

The silver pendant in Winscott's suit pocket glowed with an eerie blue light, the radiance visible even from beneath the fabric. Fallada donned his own silver pendant, a heavy sweat forming across his brow.

"No one will ever find you, Winscott," Fallada taunted, his voice now low and growling. "Not that there'll be much of you left." Fallada dropped to his hands and knees, his suit ripping at its seams as he fluidly transformed into an enormous silver-and-gray-furred wolf. The chamber door then shut on Winscott as if of its own volition, blocking his escape.

The slavering beast stalked toward Winscott from across the room. Instinctively, Winscott reached into his suit pocket and held out the pendant for protection, its unearthly light intensifying as he did.

A candescent, blue-hued fog began to seep under the closed door, engulfing the floor as the gray wolf drew closer. Fallada stopped in his—its—tracks and began to snarl, as if under attack from the spectral mists. Other wolves formed from within the fog, snapping and biting at the gray wolf. Ghostly howls echoed from the walls of the room as more wolves materialized in the vapor and besieged their beleaguered opponent.

Fallada was seized on all sides. The fog wolves pounced, clawed, bared their teeth, and finally brought down the monstrous gray wolf. The still, nude form of a man was left lying on the carpeted floor as the mists receded. Winscott leaned over Fallada's corpse, removing the silver pendant from around his neck.

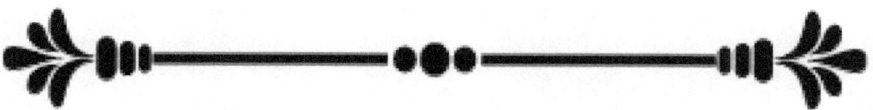

"You're not far, *señor*. You are near the castle. It's only a few miles north from here." The farmer had stopped his mule-drawn cart when Winscott hailed him. Winscott folded his map, thanked the man, and continued his journey on foot up the dusty and pitted road. He was glad to have finally found a local who could understand him this far from the city.

The imposing castle rose on the horizon, its towers jutting against a clear, blue, cloud-strewn sky. Winscott touched his shirt pocket, feeling the outline of the two pendants that rested therein. Soon, the silver pendants would be returned to the earth from which they had first been shaped, no longer the creations of men or of gods.

About the Author

James Dermond is a writer who lives in Colorado. Intrigued from a very young age by horror anthologies and the short story form, this book is his latest modest contribution to the genre.

Doorways to the Unseen 7: 6 Tales of Terror and Suspense is the seventh volume in a series of short story collections. The eighth volume in the series will be published in April 2024.

To sign up for free eBooks and other future giveaways, please subscribe to James Dermond's author website here:

www.jamesdermond.com

James Dermond's Amazon Author Page

https://www.amazon.com/James-Dermond/e/B01M1S54YP

James Dermond's Goodreads Author Page

https://www.goodreads.com/author/show/15862747.James_Dermond

James Dermond on Facebook

https://www.facebook.com/JamesDermondAuthor/

James Dermond on Twitter

JAMES DERMOND

https://twitter.com/JamesDermond

Postscript

T hank you for reading this latest volume in the short horror story series, Doorways to the Unseen! We are now on volume seven of what will eventually become a twelve-volume series of books. The planned publication schedule is two volumes for the next two years, with the final volume released in April 2026. A multi-volume hardcover edition of the collected stories would then be released in October of the same year.

If you enjoyed this collection of stories, please leave a review on Amazon and other online bookstores where volumes in the Doorways to the Unseen series can be found. A positive review will help promote the book and inform other readers of the book's merits.

www.ingramcontent.com/pod-product-compliance
Lightning Source LLC
Chambersburg PA
CBHW020423130626
46549CB00006B/2703